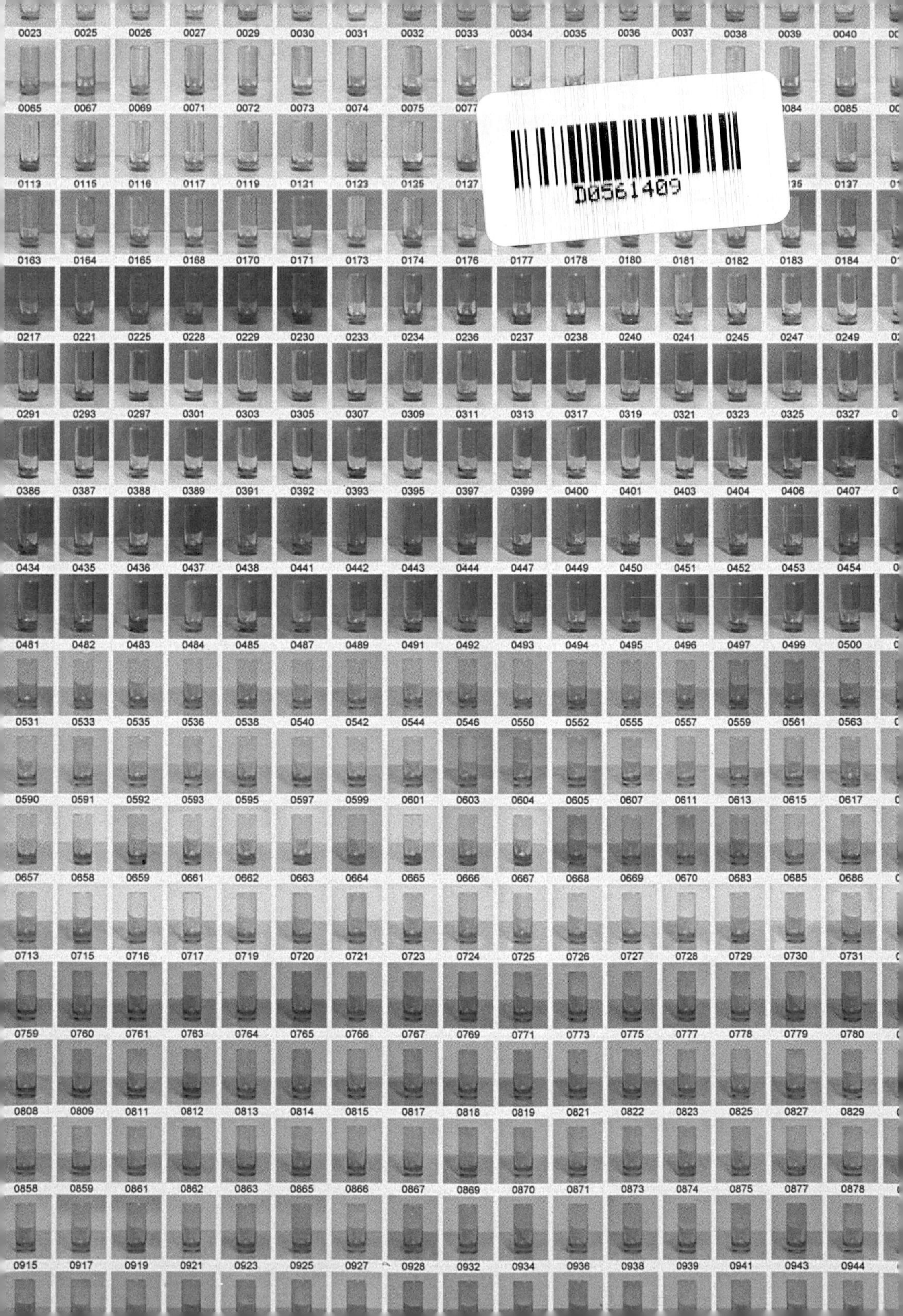
0023 0025 0026 0027 0029 0030 0031 0032 0033 0034 0035 0036 0037 0038 0039 0040
0065 0067 0069 0071 0072 0073 0074 0075 0077 0084 0085
0113 0115 0116 0117 0119 0121 0123 0125 0127 0137
0163 0164 0165 0168 0170 0171 0173 0174 0176 0177 0178 0180 0181 0182 0183 0184
0217 0221 0225 0228 0229 0230 0233 0234 0236 0237 0238 0240 0241 0245 0247 0249
0291 0293 0297 0301 0303 0305 0307 0309 0311 0313 0317 0319 0321 0323 0325 0327
0386 0387 0388 0389 0391 0392 0393 0395 0397 0399 0400 0401 0403 0404 0406 0407
0434 0435 0436 0437 0438 0441 0442 0443 0444 0447 0449 0450 0451 0452 0453 0454
0481 0482 0483 0484 0485 0487 0489 0491 0492 0493 0494 0495 0496 0497 0499 0500
0531 0533 0535 0536 0538 0540 0542 0544 0546 0550 0552 0555 0557 0559 0561 0563
0590 0591 0592 0593 0595 0597 0599 0601 0603 0604 0605 0607 0611 0613 0615 0617
0657 0658 0659 0661 0662 0663 0664 0665 0666 0667 0668 0669 0670 0683 0685 0686
0713 0715 0716 0717 0719 0720 0721 0723 0724 0725 0726 0727 0728 0729 0730 0731
0759 0760 0761 0763 0764 0765 0766 0767 0769 0771 0773 0775 0777 0778 0779 0780
0808 0809 0811 0812 0813 0814 0815 0817 0818 0819 0821 0822 0823 0825 0827 0829
0858 0859 0861 0862 0863 0865 0866 0867 0869 0870 0871 0873 0874 0875 0877 0878
0915 0917 0919 0921 0923 0925 0927 0928 0932 0934 0936 0938 0939 0941 0943 0944

This Is
NoT
IT

LYNNE TILLMAN

This Is Not It

Stories

D.A.P./DISTRIBUTED ART PUBLISHERS, INC.
NEW YORK

This is Not It: Stories by Lynne Tillman

Managing Editor: Lori Waxman
Design and typesetting: Carole Goodman/Blue Anchor Design
Printed by Palace Press in China

Published by:
D.A.P./Distributed Art Publishers, Inc.
155 Sixth Avenue, 2nd floor
New York NY, 10013
T 212.627.1999, F 212.627.9484
www.artbook.com

ISBN 1-891024-46-9

Library of Congress Cataloging-in-Publication Data
Tillman, Lynne.
This is not it : stories / by Lynne Tillman.
p. cm.
ISBN 1-891024-46-9
I. Title.
PS3570.I42 T47 2002
813'.54—dc21
2002007136

Table of Contents

For Harry Mathews

and

In memory of
Meret Oppenheim
David Rattray
Paul Bowles

COME and GO

Lynne Tillman

Peter Dreher, Tag um Tag ist guter Tag (Day by day, days are good), *1974-2002. Oil paint. Collection of the artist.*

COME AND GO

What does it matter what you say about people?
—FROM ORSON WELLES' *A TOUCH OF EVIL*

PART 1

It must have been the movie. Afterward, New Yorkers did a dumb show, and the city was silent, except for its special effects. But she heard the sinister soundtrack. Especially the hissing. Everything, everyone, was out of synch. A man with two lit cigarettes in his mouth gazed ahead, stupefied. He must've seen the movie, too.

Now it was noisy. Her head hurt in the late afternoon, when she walked up Broadway to the green market at Union Square. The fruit and vegetables looked good, but she knew she wouldn't buy any. They'd just rot. She waved her hands in the air, fending off an imaginary object or punctuating her unspoken utterances with a familiar futility. Her right hand hit a man in the shoulder. He had a stud in his ear and was carrying flowers, one of which fell to the ground. He bent to pick it up.

Charles shoved the flower into the bunch, embarrassed as hell, and the woman, whoever she was, also seemed embarrassed. He said he was sorry, though it wasn't his fault, but he always said he was sorry, and she said she was, and it was her fault, so that was right, and he walked out of the market, abandoning the profusion of ruddy people and green and yellow vegetables. Carrying flowers embarrassed him, also, as if he were in an ad for romance or Mother's Day. He touched his earring, took it out of his ear, shoved it into his pocket, annoyed about everything suddenly, noticed a cute guy on the street carrying flowers also, wondered who for, and hailed a cab.

Emma had never seen him before. He seemed to recognize her—he looked at her in the skewed way people do when they think they know you—and was gallant about being hit hard in the shoulder. But her sense of ridiculousness overcame her, and with even this brief, awkward attention, she plunged into the imaginary conversation she could fashion at the drop of a flower.

You're Emma, right?

Emma Green. Have we met?

At a party. Real name: Emerald Green?

My father was a painter and an accountant.

Weird.

Yes, Emma said, he sometimes stained his accounts.

Don't we all, she continued to herself, while the man walked off too quickly. She was a little hungry, or peckish, her English friends would say. She had not even a crumb of fantasy, not of hell or heaven, to sustain her.

Hospitals are diseased. Charles stood at the elevator, inhaling and exhaling heavily. Any elevator in a plague, he thought, and noticed three elegant male junkies—Armani suits, good haircuts—encircling a fourth, a beautiful girl they guarded like perishable treasure. The almost-dead protecting the near-dead, he thought, what Poe wished for—drop dead gorgeous. The elevator took forever. You could die waiting, someone said to someone else. Death was a grotesque punch line to this hairy ape story, an endless joke with no punch line. It had a name, but he couldn't remember it. No one ever told that kind, except his father. A shaggy dog story. He remembered the ancient phrase now, as his father's face plummeted before him, an apparition or a curtain. Next to it, a fat, wet dog shook itself violently. His father's face was wet, transparent. Rain, sweat, tears; blood, sweat, rain. The elevator arrived and two people wrapped in bandages—heads only—got off. He laughed stupidly. Couldn't help himself.

The beautiful junkie couldn't hold herself up. Without her friends, she would have gone spineless and collapsed on the floor. Third floor—drug rehab. Her friends said she had to turn herself in, be an inpatient. Hang with the in-crowd, one said drily. His eyes were tiny points. She couldn't focus. She nodded. Her body was weight. She wanted to die and had, nearly, yesterday. Or maybe it was before, in bed, but then she didn't know what

time it was or care. She wasn't thinking, she wasn't actually anything. Each one of the men holding her up, pushing her body
along, had been the object of a frail feeling, like lust but not as
energetic. Lust was dust. She hated the thick, windowless doors
that divided rehab from whatever wasn't.

Emma had seen two movies in two nights, sort of the same
movie, and afterward thought the same thought: I need a drink.
This afternoon, she went to a local bar, but a different one because
she didn't want to be seen as a woman-alone, an alcoholic, or any
of the variations or alternatives, when there were none, really.
She smiled and ordered a meal of peanuts, pretzels, and Stoli on
the rocks. A second drink produced the sensation she wanted, a
dull happiness or absence of affect, and she left, singing, not
loudly and more or less to herself, she believed. When she
reached her corner, she stepped down from the sidewalk onto
the street and into a hole. She heard a pop, began to fall, found
herself on the ground, and had to be lifted off the street by a man
she didn't know. He accompanied her to her door. Put ice on it,
he advised, keep it in the air. Maybe he was a doctor.

She didn't feel any pain, but momentarily her foot and ankle
throbbed, along with her bothersome head. Her ankle blew up.
She struggled out again, down the stairs, to the street, and pathet-
ically hailed a cab. NYU, emergency entrance, she told the driver.

The doctor's waiting room itself wanted. Anything might
enliven it, but probably not for long. A confession from the lips
of someone in much worse shape than Charles. That always gave
relief. But the air was heavy with anxiety and a damp, communal
sweat. Green walls and orange furniture. Magazines about health

or fame. He had been waiting for two hours—his doctor had been called to an emergency operation. But when the doctor walked in, finally, he'd tell Charles, I have good news. Your test result was negative. Then Charles would smile, laugh, maybe cry too. He practiced his reactions, unaware that others followed his face crumpling and relaxing. In a kind of revolving-door fantasy, the other verdict spun out: Charles, the result was positive, but don't give up hope. There are many treatments. Charles would cry then, and the doctor would offer him a tissue from a box on his desk. Charles would read the brand name and look to see if they were single or double-ply tissues. He noticed those things.

Emma hated people more today than she ever had. Her ankle pulsed, throbbed, and her heart didn't, it sank, and she was surrounded, in an ugly emergency room, by unexciting strangers. Triage meant that she wasn't a most-favored candidate for treatment, and while in most cases she'd want to be low on that list, Emma envied, in a perverse way, the startling emergencies who were taken quickly by semi-anxious professionals in white. Emergencies like the woman who'd fallen facedown on a crystal vase. Most of the professionals wore sweaters or something with a color so that the uniform wasn't uniform, and there wasn't even order to admire. Emma hated any disorder that wasn't hers. Meanwhile, with mean thoughts her company, she listened to the TV's drone; sometimes it screamed, and people paid it that curious inattention the smaller screen fosters, which, when she was feeling better or more herself, which might not be better, she liked. The new, old man next to her smelled, so she limped over to a chair near a talkative younger coot. She liked his cowboy boots.

Maggie's doctor wanted to know how she had let herself sink so low. The doctor was bald, avuncular. He followed orders and a technique meant to shake her to her senses. Boring. She looked down. Her sweater was filthy, it stuck to her body like a snake's shed skin. She was a snake. Did she really want to die? he asked. She didn't know. Probably not, she said. She didn't think she could kick, she didn't want to. Her friends were hanging around somewhere, she figured, for some news, or until it became too disgusting or sad, or they became too depressed or sick to stay. They'd split, cop, return, split, cop, return. Her parents might show up. Her mother, anyway. The same boring, angry story. She heard herself talk: I like drugs, and I'm not exceptional.

Cancer-free, Charles had himself now and no disease to battle or worry about to make his shallow life precious. He rubbed the earring he'd replaced, once he'd had the good news. He couldn't leave the hospital. It was where his father had died of cancer. Charles had an awful compulsion to stay inside the scene of his former fear and misery. He entered the dismal cafeteria, because he was hungry, he told himself, and grabbed some junk food, because he was going to live, he told himself, and sat at a table with the three elegant, druggy men, who weren't speaking and looked shaken. Stirred not shaken, he thought. Charles was content or calm. He could study, at a small distance, the faces of people like himself, who were condemned to more life.

The cowboy wasn't a cowboy, he worked in advertising, probably on that Ralph Lauren campaign, she thought. Emma's broken ankle was only a bad sprain. She was given an ace bandage, bought an aluminum cane, and her sole desire was to have her hair washed and cut. She wanted to enter the salon, don a black robe, lie down, and hear Yoji say how important hair is. Listless, she reflected for a while, then gathered her strength, rose and, balancing incorrectly on the cane, hobbled out of the hospital.

What's my name? Maggie repeated the nurse's question but thought, Turkey, cold turkey, though said, Margaret Adams. She was lying in a fog on a bed in a yellow room. She had to leave. Her friends had told her she could not sing in their group, she could not live in their loft, unless she cleaned up her act. Her mother would pay for it. Hypocrites, all of them. The nurse gave her something for the pain, and Maggie floated someplace. She noticed another person on another bed, shut her eyes again and saw a bloody hell through her eyelids. Showtime, she thought.

For a hospital cafeteria, the food wasn't bad. Charles was glad to be eating. The druggy guys interested him, as did drugs, moderately, all things in moderation. He hadn't done the hard ones, hadn't injected himself, anyway. But the lanky men barely acknowledged each other and didn't look at him. One of them finally muttered something about the beautiful, near-dead one. She was something—he couldn't catch the words—waxy, wasted, wack, worked up. The other two grunted or nodded. He supposed he wouldn't ever be even a nodding acquaintance. That amused him. Charles rubbed the ring in his ear, shook his head, and hoped to appear exotic. When no one glanced his way, he stood up, lifted his tray, as if he were partnering a great ballerina, and laughed. Then he made a slow exit. What's he on? one of the guys asked, almost interested.

It was raining hard, everyone wanted a cab, desperately. Emma didn't have an umbrella and, temporarily crippled, couldn't race for any that pulled up. She waved her cane in the air, standing on one leg like a wounded bird. It was 7:15. Maybe the salon would be open. They did models. Her hair was wet, her clothes soaked, but it didn't matter; her slight infirmity was no selling point, compared with the stricken in wheelchairs whose attendants vied near her. Suddenly a man sidled up, nodded at her with a kind of recognition—the man from the market, she remembered almost instantly—and said, I'll hail us one, how about that? Charles raced into the street and plundered the next, indifferent to the maze of wheelchair-bound. Bright eyes, a ring in his ear, he might be all right. He carried a gray attaché case and told her he made films sometimes and did PR. She'd begin with her sprained ankle.

Maggie's mother called and woke her. Though half-dead, Maggie heard the drug-induced non-anxiety coating her mother's voice.

I'm OK, Mom, she said, alive and kicking.

Very funny, her mother said.

Maggie's mother doctored film and TV scripts, especially comedies. She was not fun to live with, even when she was funny.

You mean, Maggie said, I'm not your heroine du jour.

You're not funny, her mother said.

And I'll have whatever you're having.

Her mother said she'd call later when Maggie could control herself, and Maggie rolled over, wondering if the next call would be from her father, whoever he was. Her mother, ever independent, claimed it was the man who called himself Dad, but Maggie didn't believe her. He was just her putative Pop. Pop goes the weasel.

There was an air of perfect, impossible contentment in the salon. No sound or muzak sullied the salon's minimal aesthetic. Emma and the others—men and women—received not just the salon's great cuts, but also its persuasive, osmotic sensibility. Beauty and style, like stillness, were in the air. Japanese men and women shaped and colored hair, blessed hair, of which Emma now had little. She was shorn like a sheep. Yoji colored what remained aubergine, while she contemplated Charles and their cab ride. She'd told him she was a horse trainer and had hurt her ankle in action; he'd accepted this and talked about his experience in the hospital, his relief, the junkies. Terrible crosstown traffic allowed for a long, even intimate, cab conversation. When Charles dropped her at the salon, he said he'd call—after all, they'd bumped into each other twice accidentally, didn't that mean something? She nearly said no. Now they might see each other on purpose, if he liked women, or her, which was more compli-cated. And now she had aubergine hair. She looked like an eggplant. Maybe he was partial to vegetables.

Maggie's father didn't call, until later, when Maggie was inside private hospital hell. He didn't like the idea, he told her, that she was in any institution, didn't she have friends to help her. . . . He hated hospitals, he was sick about it, her, sick sick sick. She learned he'd called her mother, to complain that Mom had driven her to drugs. Their usual fight, she told the shrink, making some inane comment about Mom having shrunk her first. Pop's involvement made her think he really was her father, but who knew. She disliked the psychiatrist, structurally speaking, but less than she had. She told him a friend of hers had OD'ed, slipping into that indefinite sleep, and she longed to have nothing to worry about, too. Her mother would say, What have you ever had to worry about?

Charles' father had been a shrink. But no talking cure for Charles—there was no talking to his father when alive, impossible dead. He threw his earring onto the dresser and lay down on the floor. He stretched idly. He masturbated and thought afterward about the first time he'd had an erection—sitting on the chair his mother loved. That was such a dopey memory, he wept. He ordered Chinese food, watched Bill Murray in *What about Bob?* and fell into a comfortable nostalgia. His father had never had a stalker patient like Bob. But to his father, Charles could have been a Bob. He'd never know.

Emma's hair, in the light, was even more purple, but it would fade, everything fades. Yoji had done the best he could, his best was better than most, but he didn't understand lavender. She didn't understand people's love of purple prose, she preferred porn, but there was none in her apartment. The light by her bed was not strong enough, the phone by her bed did not ring enough. It sat on the table like a dumpy Buddha. Her older sister had told her, all her life, that she had a big mouth. Emma didn't think that was true. She wasn't nasty, just frank, candid as a camera, which also, like her, lied. She looked different in every photo she took.

PART 2

The next morning, when Charles went to work, he was determined
to overcome a recalcitrant melancholy. Charles was a publicist, and
he worked hard to sound on top of things. I'm on top of things,
don't worry, he'd say. He handled a range of clients from foundations to individuals and was moderately successful, giving good
phone, demanding without seeming obsequious or needy. Sounding
needy was bad, only for the last resort, and some of his clients were.
This morning, when he hailed a taxi, he remembered the horse
trainer from the hospital and their weird ride together. He decided
he'd call her, she seemed sympathetic if neurotic. Charles phoned
immediately. Otherwise he might not. Sometimes he was impulsive.
His impulses were, he thought, the best thing about him.

Emma woke to his early morning call. They should be banned,
she thought, except that they might contain early warnings
and be necessary, but then that's why they were horrible and
should be banned. Charles was in a taxi again.

You get around early, she said.

Don't you go to work? he said.

Work comes to me.

She yawned, purposefully.

Want to explain that? Charles asked.

No, Emma said.

He laughed, which was OK, and she agreed to meet him at
the Oyster Bar the next night. Thinking of oysters made her sick,
but she superimposed Charles' face on the slimy creatures.
Maybe he wasn't as slimy.

Maggie's dreamlife worked overtime to produce excessive colors and danger. She slept as much as she could. Though given to dramatic sighs and moans, she was no 19th-century heroine. She cursed her fate, her so-called life, and filled it now with an aggressive, contemptuous self-pity. She was in a room with three people, all of whom were, like her, withdrawing and in the program. She felt compelled to muffle herself. She was withdrawn, anyway, and withdrew further, to stay inside herself. The drug was out of her system. But her brain kept its vivacious memory to which she, her body or her brain, achingly returned. Shit. Each day her roommates became less loathsome to her; and she wasn't sure why. She feared she might be turned, like a trick, into a loathsome Pollyanna. Her best friend assured her that was impossible. That's what best friends were for.

"Even though," Charles contended, fixing the ear piece of his phone, "even if you did all the work and he's taking the credit, it doesn't matter, because you'll still get paid." Assuaging a client's hurt feelings, encouraging the wounded ego to roll with a career's punk punches, was what he was paid for. Charles sometimes believed the lies or relative truths he insisted upon. How crazy everything is, he'd sometimes declare. And it was. Everything. Crazy. Still, when he hung up the phone and looked out of his office window at other office windows, Charles' body collapsed a little, let down by something he could never name. The light was leaving, and something with promise was snatched away, or it was the beginning of darkness and the start of unnameable feelings. He should work late, but he had a date with Emma, whatever she was or did, at six. Her work came to her, she had said, mysteriously. Analyst, personal trainer? Oysters on the half shell with a strange woman might be just what the doctor ordered, although he couldn't remember any doctor saying anything like that.

In group therapy, following a hostile silence, Maggie told everyone what she thought of them. They in turn told her. No one liked her. She didn't care. The opinion of one woman affected her, mostly because it was offered with discernment and haughty disdain. Maggie decided to win her. It was a junkie's form of sublimation—to score the love or good feeling of the most truculent, the most obdurate. Someone like herself. Someone desirable for all the wrong reasons, who suffered as she did from helplessness. No one liked her, but she wasn't going to eat worms. She could be charming. She'd turn it on.

Titillated by the evening's possibilities, Emma energetically, or libidinally, she might ironically put it, threw herself into her job. She was a social worker and psychic. Emma had wanted to become a psychoanalyst and determinedly entered into training after receiving her MSW. Along the way she developed an unfortunate transference to her training analyst—she thought he was trying to destroy her. Much as he tried to convince her this was a projection, when one of his other analysands committed suicide, Emma's fears were confirmed. As a social worker, she was licensed to treat individual patients; and her psychic powers were something that, over the years, she'd come to use and trust. Slowly she had brought them into her practice, with the right patients, and slowly word spread among the unhappy and the chic that Emma absolutely saw right through you, as if you were glass, to the inside or the other side. It was peculiar to Emma that she herself was unlucky in love, but like the esteemed editor who can't write, Emma spotted the problem because it wasn't hers.

Maggie's obdurate woman—the woman least likely to succumb, to her—had skin like mother of pearl. Like my mother's old compact, Maggie thought. The woman's pearlescence was the first reason Maggie stared at her. Then it was her airy disinterest. Maggie soon wanted the woman's good opinion, though it signaled a corruption of her usual state of mind. But Maggie was out of her mind, out of it. One of the nurses repeated several times that quitting junk was easier than stopping smoking. Her stained fingers and teeth were a burnt testament to that truth. The obdurate one, smoking in a corner, coughed and laughed. Bitter humor smoothed Maggie's serrated edges. She took it for sophistication. Being sophisticated, Maggie felt, established a respectable distance from the unhappy pursuit of happiness.

When Charles and Emma met at the Oyster Bar, Emma didn't see right through him and he didn't understand her. It was the source of their immediate attraction. She admitted she didn't train horses and didn't explain why she had lied initially. Her refusal to explain was itself seductive; Charles never wanted to and thrilled to those who didn't, imagining they possessed an inner grace. From Emma's viewpoint, Charles' hunger to be liked and his cuteness—the earring he kept tugging—were undercut by his reticence. She took shyness for truthfulness. Disingenuous herself, she was susceptible to people who hadn't given up on honesty's promise. They usually were promising.

The next time they met, Charles kissed Emma, after two bottles of Taittingers. He opened his mouth completely, his wet, upper lip clinging to the tip of her nose. If he was gay, she thought, he was very generous. The more they touched each other, the more they liked each other, a feeling neither could remember having had in a while. Aroused, Emma asked him what he liked best. When Charles said, Honestly, sweetie, I don't know, she almost fainted.

Nothing nothing mattered. Nothing. Nothing nothing mattered. He was on top of the world, his world. Nothing mattered, he was shattered. What about Charles, Charles? he bellowed in the shower, lathering again and again, getting clean clean clean. Skin is thin, sin is fat, it's like that. He pinched himself. He wanted to cancel every appointment, because nothing mattered, but then he buttoned his jacket, picked up his keys, and strolled to the subway. Mass transit. He hadn't had sex—say LOVE, Charles—since he thought he was dying. Now he knew he wasn't—say LIFE, Charles—nothing really mattered, nothing nothing. He'd send Emma flowers and buy a new bed, throw out the old, full of sorrows, toss out every Tom, Dick, Harriette and Charlene who'd rolled there. A firm bed. FUN, Charles, nothing mattered so much you couldn't have fun. And weren't Metro cards great, too.

Dr. Bones, Maggie named him, was gaunt, like a user, except some junkies were fat. Bones expected her to talk and talk five times a week, which was how you knew she was in a watering hole for wealthy abusers and other rich, dependent types. Women who loved gross men and forced them into dresses, men who chased women who despised men. It catered to the best of the worst. Bones was handsome, in a tortured way, with rings under his eyes, one for every sad story he heard. She liked that. He was perceptive, or maybe there wasn't much hidden. The obdurate one wasn't talking in group, just staring, still pearly, and sometimes laughing through her opaque eyes. Maggie talked to Bones about her. He said Maggie's fantasies were analyzable. Analyze that? Maggie sighed.

Emma's dilemma wasn't Charles, not in the purest sense, though nothing was innocent. She hadn't liked someone in a long time and was unused to it. Charles was returning tonight—"I can't get enough of you"—and she was glad, she thought. But her life already had a shape she liked, its dimensions assured her. She could make a list and follow it. Apart from an accident, when she landed in an emergency room and met a man like Charles, life conformed to her expectations. Nothing extraordinary. That might seem strange given her psychic powers, but it wasn't to her. There were no great surprises. People were unhappy and wanted confirmation they were right; that the pain wouldn't last long, and in the end they'd be loved and rich. Happiness would discover them as if it were a talent scout, and doesn't everyone have talent. Charles had sent flowers twice. His enthusiasm overflowed. Emma wondered what his story was. Last night he phoned once, then twice, but later she turned off the ringer.

Maggie didn't answer her calls now.

Charles didn't want to speak to anyone except Emma.

Emma was exhausted.

PART 3

They didn't want to be themselves, they wanted to be someone else. If they weren't themselves, they weren't anyone else, either. Who they should have been, they never imagined they could be. And then, as if by magic or the stroke of a sword or pen, they vanished.

With that, I came into being.

I wanted them to go, and I have my reasons. The disappearance of Charles and Emma resulted from a fast, ferocious pull toward each other that could have just one end—as strong a repulsion. Maggie withdrew from drugs and entered therapy like Alice falling through a hole in the ground. She had grown so little, her withdrawal was complete.

I had seen myself, or expressed myself, to be old-fashioned, in them, since Charles, Emma, and Maggie were excrescences of my needs, evidence of my frailties. I used them, too, but because I can be frivolous and intellectually promiscuous—I flirt whenever I can with whatever I can—their usefulness stopped. My interest in them as extensions of myself has, too, and now I don't want to need them. I'd like to be myself. I'm not sure what that means, but I think it signifies an oppressive self-centeredness.

I left them before they left me.

I shift between wishing to control what I can and being afraid I will, only to become bored, and vacillate between a dislike of constancy and consistency and the fear that I will inevitably be betrayed by others who lose interest and float away. We are things bobbing in the water, things to be discarded when advantage has been taken and regard lost.

I'm not inured to myself, but on some days I think I am. Hating yourself is a thankless job, and others can relieve you of the obligation. People are more easily defined by those who hate them than by those who love them. Sadly, the people who hate me are weak and vile. But I don't court disaster; it visits me. I don't flaunt, I don't shout on streets or on buses. I've been a good dog in the backseat of the big family car. My tongue never hangs out, I don't slobber and drool, I don't piss on the seat. I curb myself until I can't stand it anymore.

Charles, Emma, and Maggie are figments, elements. I couldn't bear to be them, and maybe I am them. I'm not everyman. I'm no one in particular, and they're not just clutter, my trash or dust bunnies. But I do sweep, collect, and hurl bits and pieces into the whirly world.

I miss them already.

Yesterday I was determined to remake myself into any appealing image. I watched TV. *Dances with Wolves* was on, and I wanted to be the Indian woman when she was slashing herself after her mate's death and also the wolf on the plain. A combination of their passion and fierceness, with the wolf and Indian woman emblematic of my person, would form the design for the fearsome, inviolate character of my dreams. In dreams begin what?

Everything challenges the tenuous world order. Every emotion derails every other one. One rut is disrupted by the emergence of another. I began drinking white wine, had a thirst for it, and now demand it at 6 p.m., exactly, as if my life depended upon it. That was a while ago.

What does a life depend upon?

Maggie is a handy composite of some people I've loved whose narcissism was once irresistible. When you fall out of love with a narcissist, life is emptier. The real M and I have known each other a while. If she opened any of my notebooks and saw how I see her, she would be displeased—but also glumly appreciative. At least I thought of her. M thrives on the way I help her, on how I support or serve her, and I lean on that.

What am I serving, and who, I ask myself, a glass of white wine—it's 6 p.m., the light's leaving—in my hand. The wine's subtle, from Umbria. Take umbrage, I tell myself.

Whose will do I bend to, and from whom do I beg forgiveness so quietly I'm never heard? With its remarkable colors and aftertastes, the wine, dry as wit, urges me to forgive myself.

Life's aim, Freud thought, was death. I can't know this, but maybe it's death I want. Life comes with its own exigencies, like terror.

The notebooks I mentioned don't exist. I wish I kept a running account of my life—then the complaints and pleasures wouldn't be forgotten, by me. I'd like, at the end of a year, to be able to read a detailed ledger of time past, to be able to linger in, even relive, all my days, one by one, and by paying attention to time, also obliterate it.

I don't have this kind of attention, I don't live a life of calm reflection, I don't add up the days, I don't make good use of time, I waste a lot of it, and it wastes me, and I'm not sure each day counts, although I also think it may, with frightening consequences. I have a memory that usually doesn't fail, unless recording pain involuntarily is a failure.

The actual Emma prides herself on her memory. She often flaunts her great gift. In an argument about the past, recent mostly, she details an incident with a flourish, displaying it like a precious jewel from a former lover. She has a good memory, and she has many souvenirs.

These days are Emma's. Memory is what everyone talks about. Will we remember, and what will we remember, who won't be mentioned, or who will be written out, ignored, obliterated.

I didn't decide to forget.

People make lists, take vitamins, and exercise. It's reported that brain cells don't die. I never believed they did. The tenaciousness of memory, its viciousness really—witness the desire over history for revenge—has forever been a sign that the brain recovers. I remember too much and too little.

Try to hang on to what you can. It's really going. So am I.

Someone else's biography seems like my life. I read it and confuse it with my own. I watch a movie, convinced it happened to me. I suppose it did happen to me. I don't know what I think anymore, and I don't know what I don't think.

I'm someone who tells things.

I'm more or less like Charles. He makes me giddy with possibility, the sense that nothing is impossible. Cocaine also does this. Charles didn't have cancer, so I will never have it. I am a man unsure of himself with women. Every flight and fancy is riddled with openings to vaults storing unacknowledged or hidden lusts. But I'm not sure if desire is naked. Grifters seduce suckers so fast; they know how to dress up their leechlike plans. Some days it's all I can see—the scheme residing on the surface, or located in a gesture, the terrified glance, or the traitorous word not spoken.

But where does all this lead, where does this suspiciousness get me?

I wanted to locate movie footage of tidal waves. They occurred in typical dreams. But an oceanographer told me that a tidal wave was a tsunami, it moved under the ocean and couldn't be seen. This bothered me for a long time. I wondered what it was that destroyed whole villages, just washed them away.

Maggie might think that. Maybe she did, and I stole it. There are people who think they're being stolen from all the time. Generally, they have nothing anyone wants. Maggie's absorbing addiction to heroin—I almost wrote heroine—is a physical attachment and an embodiment of neediness, repugnant because of that. She is also romantically engaged with the underground, unseen creature in her that moves through the world and crashes on someone else's floor, destroying everything around it and her.

That's dramatic. Maybe I'm trapped in a new romanticism. After midnight, there are parties, the music's thunderous, and we perform excessive, heartbreaking dances of sex and love. I fly across the floor, leap into the air, and catch myself. I have to rescue myself everywhere.

This morning's decision: let life rush over me. The recurring tidal wave is not about sexual thralldom, not the spectacular orgasm, not the threat of dissolution and loss of control through sex—that, too—but a wish to be overcome by life rather than to run it. To be overrun.

Running away, I make things up—Emma, Charles, Maggie. I want to have them again, I want to live with them. I don't believe any response, like invention, is sad. The world is made up of imagining. I imagine this, too.

Things circle now, all is flutter. Things fall down and rise up. Hope and remorse, beauty and viciousness, and imagination, wherever it doggedly hides, unveil petulant realities.

I live in my mind, and I don't.

There's scant privacy for bitterness or farting or the inexpressible; historically, there was an illusion of privacy. Illusions are necessary.

The wretched inherit what no one wants.

In the beginning, the woman in the green market became Emma, but naming her was a dubious activity. She was a thought, who had to be called something in order to exist.

What separates me from the world? Secret thoughts?

I produce a lot of garbage, and I'm not alone, I see it piling up on sidewalks. It could, one day, overwhelm the city. I can picture it. But sometimes I dismiss my fantasy life, and then I can't fantasize. This augurs a terrible constipation—a walling in, holing up, dropping out of sight, believing stuff must be kept inside, held there, wherever that is. It's too disgusting to release. Let go and what comes out is shit.

Maggie has just left rehab, riding the same elevator down that she took on her way up. Two of the guys are waiting in the lobby. They're clean, they say.

Emma phones Charles from a taxi, where she always thinks about him, when she thinks about him. Each time she decides she's over him, she realizes she's not. There's something about him.

Charles hears her voice coming out of a small, black box. He tugs on his earring. He reaches for the phone. His hand wavers over the receiver.

Everything is a decision now.

What Americans fear is the inability to have a world different from their father's and mother's. That's why we move so much, to escape history.

Margaret Fuller said: I accept the universe.

I try to embrace it. But I will leave it to others to imagine the world in ways I can't.

I leave it to others.

Out of nothing comes language and out of language comes nothing and everything. I know there will be stories. Certainly, there will always be stories.

madame
REALISM

Lynne Tillman

Kiki Smith, Madame Realism, *1984. Ink on paper.*
Courtesy of Kiki Smith and Lynne Tillman.

MADAME REALISM

Madame Realism read that Paul Eluard had written: No one has divined the dramatic origin of teeth. She pictured her dentist, a serious man who insisted gravely that he alone had saved her mouth.

The television was on. It had been on for hours. Years. It was there. TV on demand, a great freedom. Hadn't Burroughs said there was more freedom today than ever before. Wasn't that like saying things were more like today than they've ever been.

Madame Realism heard the announcer, who didn't know he was on the air, say: Hello, victim. Then ten seconds of nothing, a commercial, the news, and *The Mary Tyler Moore Show*.

She inhaled her cigarette fiercely, blowing the smoke out hard. The television interrupts itself: A man wearing diapers is running around parks, scaring little children. The media call him Diaperman.

The smoke and her breath made a whooshing sound that she liked, so she did it again and again. When people phoned she blew right into the receiver, so that she sounded like she was panting.

Smokers, she read in a business report, are less productive than nonsmokers, because they spend some of their work time staring into space as they inhale and exhale. She could have been biding her time or protecting it. All ideas are married.

He thought she breathed out so deeply to let people know she was there. Her face reminded him, he said, of a Japanese movie. She didn't feel like talking, the telephone demanded like an infant not yet weaned. Anything can be a transitional object. No one spoke of limits, they spoke of boundaries. And my boundaries shift, she thought, like ones do after a war when countries lose or gain depending upon having won or lost. Power has always determined right.

Overheard: A young mother is teaching her son to share his toys, the toys he really cares about. There are some things you can call your own, he will learn. Boundaries are achieved through battle.

Madame Realism was not interested in display. Men fighting in bars, their nostrils flaring and faces getting red, their noses filling with mucous and it dripping out as they fought over a pack of cigarettes, an insult, a woman. But who could understand men, or more, what they really wanted.

Dali's conception of sexual freedom, for instance, written in 1930. A man presenting his penis "erect, complete, and magnificent plunged a girl into a tremendous and delicious confusion, but without the slightest protest. . . . It is," he writes, "one of the purest and most disinterested acts a man is capable of performing in our age of corruption and moral degradation."

She wondered if Diaperman felt that way. Just that day a beggar had walked past her. When he got close enough to smell him, she read what was written on his button. It said BE APPROPRIATE. We are like current events to each other. One doesn't have to know people well to be appropriate.

Madame Realism is at a dinner party surrounded by people, all of whom she knows, slightly. At the head of the table is a silent woman who eats rather slowly. She chooses a piece of silverware as if it were a weapon. But she does not attack her food.

One of the men is depressed; two of his former lovers are also at the dinner. He thinks he's Kierkegaard. One of his former lovers gives him attention, the other looks at him ironically, giving him trouble. A pall hangs over the table thick like stale bread. The silent woman thinks about death, the expected. Ghosts are dining with us.

A young man, full of the literature that romanticizes his compulsion, drinks himself into stupid liberation. He has not yet discovered that the source of supposed fictions is the desire never to feel guilty.

The depressed man thinks about himself, and one of the women at the table he hasn't had. This saddens him even more. At the same time it excites him. Something to do—to live for—at the table. Wasn't desire for him at the heart of all his, well, creativity?

He becomes lively and sardonic. Madame Realism watches his movements, listens to what he isn't saying, and waits. As he gets the other's attention, he appears to grow larger. His headache vanishes with her interest. He will realize that he hadn't had a headache at all. Indifferent to everyone but his object of the moment, upon whom he thrives from titillation, he blooms. Madame Realism sees him as a plant, a wilting plant that is being watered.

The television glowed, effused at her. Talk shows especially encapsulated America, puritan America. One has to be seen to be doing good. One has to be seen to be good. When he said a Japanese movie, she hadn't responded. Screens upon screens and within them. A face is like a screen when you think about the other, when you think about projection. A mirror is a screen and each time she looked into it, there was another screen test. How did she look today? What did she think today? Isn't it funny how something can have meaning and no meaning at the same time.

Madame Realism read from *The New York Times:* "The Soviet Ambassador to Portugal had formally apologized for a statement issued by his embassy that called Mario Soares, the Socialist leader, a lunatic in need of prolonged psychiatric treatment. The embassy said the sentence should have read 'these kinds of lies can only come from persons with a sick imagination, and these lies need prolonged analysis and adequate treatment.'" Clever people plot their lives with strategies not unlike those used by governments. We all do business. And our lies are in need of prolonged analysis and adequate treatment.

When the sun was out, it made patterns on the floor, caused by the bars on her windows. She liked the bars. She had designed them. Madame Realism sometimes liked things of her own design. Nature was not important to her; the sun made shadows that could be looked at and about which she could write. After all, doesn't she exist, like a shadow, in the interstices of argument.

Her nose bled for a minute or two. Having needs, being contained in a body, grounded her in the natural. But even her period appeared with regularity much like a statement from the bank. Madame Realism lit another cigarette and breathed in so deeply, her nose bled again.

I must get this fixed, she thought, as if her nostrils had brakes. There is no way to compare anything. We must analyze our lives. There isn't even an absolute zero. What would be a perfect sentence?

A turn to another channel. The night was cold, but not because the moon wasn't out. The night was cold. She pulled her blanket around her. It's cold but it's not as cold as simple misunderstanding that turns out to run deep. And it's not as cold as certain facts: She didn't love him, or he her; hearts that have been used badly. Experience teaches not to trust experience. We're forced to be empiricists in bars.

She looked into the mirror. Were she to report that it was cracked, one might conjure it, or be depressed by a weak metaphor. The mirror is not cracked. And stories do not occur outside thought. Stories, in fact, are contained within thought. It's only a story really should read, it's a way to think.

Madame Realism turned over and stroked her cat, who refused to be held longer than thirty seconds. That was a record. She turned over and slept on her face. She wondered what it would do to her face but she slept that way anyway, just as she let her body go and didn't exercise, knowing what she was doing was not in her interest. She wasn't interested. It had come to that. She turned off the television.

Lynne Tillman

to find words

Stephen Prina, Untitled, Version I, *1987. Graphic marker dye on drafting film, mahogany, rag board. 24⁵/₁₆ x 20¹³/₁₆ inches. Private collection.*

TO FIND WORDS

The mechanism of poetry is the same as that of hysterical phantasies.

—SIGMUND FREUD

I have nothing to say. There is nothing to say is another way to say it. Or, still another way, there is so much to say, and so many ways, should I begin? May I begin? Do I need to ask your permission? I promise you delight. I promise you a real good time. I promise you the best. This will be the very best, the best you've ever had. I am a ride, a roller coaster, the fun house. I'm what frightens you in the palace of horror. I'm pleasure. I'm a drive in the backseat of a car late at night when the moon is full and everyone else is asleep. I'm sex. I'm compassion. I'm the tears on your cheek when you say goodbye forever to that handsome but pitiful character in the movie you love. Now I'm anger and outrage, fire engine red inside your brain. I'm choking you with rage. I'm the pain that dwells in your gut which you cannot express to anyone. I'm the ache in your heart. It hurts. You hurt. You cannot speak. Lie down, make yourself comfortable, adjust the light. I'll speak for you.

That's the problem. And I could go this way or that, tell this story or that. I could seem to believe in words, I could pretend to believe in words and in the power of stories. I could insist: I am a storyteller. I could take comfort in conventional wisdoms and make many references, shoring up my position, to defend myself to you and from you. I could hate words, distrust language, forego stories. I could do all this, everything. I could use everything, I could try it all.

I could, but I don't want to. I don't care, though that's not entirely true. It is partially true and partial truths are after all what one must settle for. If one settles. I don't know about you, but I feel like hell. The country is falling apart, what does anything matter, people are dying, starving, being blown out of the sky, people are suffering, and what does anything matter, what difference does this nothing make, what matter do words make?

When she awoke, she could not speak at all. I didn't let her swallow, she felt she could not breathe, her throat was dry, she drank many glasses of water, she went back to bed and fretted silently. Words danced in front of her, a ballet that no one would comprehend. This word partners that? She could not swallow, that damned, fucking, horrible lump in her throat. It is not the first time. It happens often. Such a weird sensation.

It's terrible that I am her voice because she depends on me. She is to be pitied. She looks sad, lying there in her mother's nightgown. Her mother is dead. Suddenly she sits up, puts a notebook on her lap, and finds a pen on the floor, the pen she threw away last night (oh last night). She writes in her notebook. Her other hand is wrapped lightly about her throat as if she were gagging herself.

The Body has a Mind of its Own
The Mind Speaks through its Body
The Body Speaks its Mind
The Mind has a Body of its Own

"To write a story is to be in a state of hysteria. Writers call up from their minds and bodies (I do not make a separation) memories, ideas, fragments of thoughts, images. The fragmented story is symptomatic, and like a symptom of the hysteric, who cannot retrieve the whole, it is stymied by a regrettable and important loss from a particular scene that would make the story complete. But even the narrative that we think of as well-formed, the traditional narrative, with a beginning, middle and end, that too is of necessity a fragment, which he writer, to counter loss, is impelled to produce. All writing is hysterical. The body always speaks."

This was the voice that Paige Turner initially chose, from many possible voices, I might add, to begin a story about hysteria. She had studied and studied, thought and thought, and from all that she had read, and from all that was in her, so to speak. Paige decided to sally forth with a jab at the problem of writing itself. It is one possible approach. Sally go round the roses.

It doesn't seem to me that it is exactly the right voice or precisely the right way to begin. The first line of a story is like the first impression one can never make again. You never get a second chance to make a first impression. I am not completely sure and neither is she. And it is this that I have reminded her: Is this your voice? Couldn't anyone else have written this? Who is speaking? And, of course, who cares?

Paige Turner is a tall woman, with bright red hair. She is a petite woman with jet black hair. She is of middling height, has blond hair and is known to diet strenuously and laugh loudly. Today her cough is constant; she hates what she has written. She will not begin her story that way, but it will plague her. Paige worries that the ideas she thinks urgent won't be understood. On the other hand overstatement worries her more. She thinks this and glances at her other hand. There is dirt under two of her nails. Red nail polish peels off both thumbnails. Her hands look injured, as if they've been to war. She will apply more red polish to her short, dirty nails. One hand is shaking. This is beyond her control.

When Paige was just a child, she would shake at the kitchen table, shake her leg so vigorously that her father would joke: Will that be a chocolate or a vanilla milk shake? Paige shakes her head, to forget the moment and his expression, what he said as well as the look on his face. A look of bemusement, mockery or tenderness. The look that she remembers, the look she invents again and again, is a jumble in her mind which she thinks of as a kind of messy store where her trinkets and junk are displayed, where other people's souvenirs, other people's pasts, are represented, all as small objects. Precious memory. Her throat hurts. She swallows hard. She cannot speak.

I call her Little Miss Understood. Naming is everything. Sticks and stones will break your bones and names will always hurt you. Names will make you cry. A comic and ominous taunt to Little Miss Understood sitting at her Underwood. On days that are wet and grey or on bright blue ones, it drives her crazy. Mad, wack, nuts, bonkers, ape shit, and so on. I drive her out of her mind. She wants to do the driving herself. She walks back and forth mumbling aloud, speaking to herself. She tells herself that it is a mark of intelligence to talk to oneself—she read this in a popular psychology column written by Dr. Joyce Brothers, for *Vogue* magazine. She takes comfort in such reassurances. She sits at her desk, pulls at her hair, jerks her leg and sorts through paper. She opens books and stares into space. She looks at old photographs of herself and her family, of lovers and friends. Sometimes she imagines she is staring inward, as when she pretends that the outside is the inside. Have you ever tried that? At other times she gazes at the pictures on her walls to invigorate her mind, to catch herself unaware, to startle herself with new meanings. There is a lump in her throat.

"I look for a hair that might have lodged between my lips when eating. It has been swallowed and sits in my throat, tickling me, tickling my fancy. I have eaten hair. Disgusting? Disgust is interesting. Voices can be disgusting. Insinuating, dirty. A voice from the past. I will tell the dirty old man story. Every woman has a dirty old man story."

She is hoarse, her voice deep in her raw throat. But she begins to write, which I think takes pluck, shows stubbornness or demonstrates a kind of silliness, a deep silliness deep in her deep throat. I ought not trivialize the task before her, but how can I not? I remind her how foolish she is. She glances at the ceiling, distracted. She touches her throat and coughs. She calls to me, her disembodied voice. Be still, lie down, rise up, die, live.

"She was sick to her stomach. The bus ride was supposed to take five hours, but it was raining and the slick roads caused the driver to go slowly. Time was dragging, moving along with the labored swish of the window wipers. Time was dumb and slow. She liked buses better than trains because the lights were always off in buses if you rode late enough at night. She was returning to college. She'd eaten so much during the weekend at home that she could barely move. She opened the button at the top of her pants. Her mother had made a chocolate cake which she'd finished when her family had gone to bed. She vomited in the morning but she knew she'd gained weight anyway.

"The man next to her stirred. He'd been sleeping since the beginning of the trip. Now he was awake. He was old and his face was covered by stubble. He was fat too. He started to talk to her. He ran a fast-food chicken place on Second Avenue, he asked if she'd ever been there. She said no. She was glad to talk even though he was ugly. In the light he would be even uglier so she was glad it was dark in the bus. After a while she didn't know what else to talk about because she didn't think he'd be interested in what she was studying or the fact that one day she was going to be a writer. She was too self-conscious to say any of it anyway. It seemed stupid.

"So she closed her eyes. She covered herself with her coat and pretended to go to sleep. He didn't do anything for a while. Then he placed his hand on her pants, first on her thigh, and then he moved his hand there. He began to rub her. No one had ever done that. She didn't know what to do. She didn't think she wanted him to stop because the feeling was strange and nice. She knew it was wrong but it didn't matter what it was. She watched the feelings she was having. She felt very far away. Then she became more and more uncomfortable. She felt hotter. She pretended to wake up and went to the bathroom. There are always bathrooms on Greyhound buses. Everyone else was asleep. She was really alone. Inside the small toilet she felt her underpants. They were wet. She went back to her seat and told the dirty old man, 'I know what you were doing and it was wrong. Don't do it again.' The words came from outside of her, as if spoken by an intruder. It was a strange voice, almost unrecognizable."

I disgust her. She returns to bed. She is discontented. The story may not be right, the voice off. Unsure, she shrinks from herself. She is too little to live. To love. She is too big. There is no time to be content. I disgust her. The hair tickles her throat, her fancy. Her fancy is a lump in her throat.

The saying, I have a lump in my throat, is used generally, in English anyway, when someone feels a great burst of sad emotion, a swelling of emotion. Emotion seems to swell and gets stuck in the body, odd though that may be. The swelling becomes physical, something is stuck in one's throat. Often I become a thing in her throat, as if she'd swallowed a great obstacle and it lodged there. I don't mean she actually swallowed an obstacle. I mean I am the lump in her throat, which is an obstacle. As she writes the dirty old man story, she loses her voice—a case of laryngitis. She cannot speak above a whisper. She wonders if her loss is also her gain, one voice for another. She wonders if she is a whispering woman. She coughs.

"A woman I know attended a private screening of a film. Jackie Kennedy Onassis entered the small cinema, with another woman. Jackie Onassis stood close to my friend who was sitting at the end of the row. She had never seen Jackie O. in person. It was peculiar because she felt she had grown up with her. Jackie O. had recently had a facelift and she looked much younger than she was. That was peculiar too. Jackie O. whispered loudly to her friend, who had red hair and was as tall as she. The whisper was a stage whisper. It could be heard all through the room. When the two sat down in front, Jackie O. kept whispering, her head inclined close to her friend's. But when the movie started, she stopped and sat absolutely still in her seat, not moving. Not once during the entire movie did she move. She was fixed in her seat. That too was strange. The movie ended and Jackie O. and her friend walked out behind my friend. Jackie O. was still whispering.

Afterward there was a lavish reception. My friend took a seat on a couch and drank wine. She saw Jackie O. talking to some people. My friend thought, I'm glad not to be introduced to her. What could I possibly say to her? Later she mentioned this to her lover. He said, 'You could have asked her if she saw anything on the grassy knoll.' They laughed for a long time, imagining how Jackie O. might respond. They knew she wouldn't. I told my friend I'd once heard that Mary Todd Lincoln also whispered. But whether she whispered after Lincoln's assassination or whether she whispered all her life, I didn't know.

"The next day I read in *The New Yorker* magazine about a woman who had placed her mother in a nursing home. The woman's mother warned her, 'If you do this to me, you'll never sleep again.' The woman developed insomnia on the day her mother entered the home. She has not slept regularly since."

Paige might call this The Whispering Women. I remind her that the mother did not warn her daughter, You will lose your power of speech or stutter for the rest of her life. That would be germane. But Paige likes the insomnia story. It gives her goosebumps just to think of it. It makes her flesh crawl. It makes her look behind her to see if someone is standing there. She has a coughing fit. She is thinking and she is not thinking. She may be dreaming.

Paige's mother is in a nursing home. On the day she left her there, and after parting from the reluctant, tearful, elderly woman, Paige came down with the flu. It turned into strep throat. And she lost her voice. Who could she have talked to about it anyway, she thought.

   To find words, to find words from all the possible words. It's
a game, like Stick the Tail on the Donkey or Treasure Hunt. The
hunt may or may not offer a reward at its conclusion. The game
cannot be Monopoly. You know that. To find words and place
them in sentences in a certain order. Syntax.

"There is a sin tax in the U.S. on liquor and cigarettes, on luxuries,
but what are luxuries. What isn't necessary and who decides that?"

If I let her find words, she will rush to form sentences. She will
rush to judgment and will try to make sense. Can she?

She persists. Sense and nonsense. Words free, unfixed. Paige longs
to make music with words, to discover the moment when words
vibrated in the body. She wants to discover time inside herself,
to give rhythm to her sentences. Style is rhythm. Rhythm is
style. She hears a drumbeat, then a bass line, tough and funky.
She imagines the inside is the outside. She is greedy for everything. She opens her mouth wide. If words could make wishes
come true. If wishes were horses she'd ride away. Paige wants a
voice like the wind.
   I tell her: The wind has a voice but I cannot mimic it. The
wind has its own music. The wind howls, everyone says so. It is
a wolf. I cannot be a wolf. I cannot howl. When I give voice to
a thought—do you like that?— it may sound scratchy. Her voice
may sound thin, a scream vibrating at a frequency unbearable to
dogs or wolves. Do you find that amusing? I had to urge those
words from the local box into the mouth and onto the tongue.

She repeats them. Her tongue is pink and whitish and scalloped at the edges. She is neither proud nor ashamed of her tongue. She can't touch her chin with her tongue. She rarely thinks of her tongue but when she does, she begins to imagine that her tongue is too large for her mouth. When she realizes this feeling, she gets small sores on the sides of her tongue. Then she remembers her mother telling her, when she was little, Don't get too big for your britches. Paige didn't know exactly what britches were, then.

"I dreamed that I was a man who was a psychoanalyst. We were sitting in a circle, I was opposite him. There were other people in the circle, too. He told me that he had been looking up my skirt. He spoke indifferently. I said to him indignantly, surprised, 'I'm used to wearing pants, not skirts. I am very angry that you continued to look up my skirt and didn't warn me.'"

Her sister takes her to a shopping mall which turns into a medieval castle. Paige doesn't remember this part of the dream. Anyway, if she publishes it, it's not her dream anymore. She shakes her head, rubs her eyes, pours a cup of tea and has the sense—sensation settling in her throat, words are stuck there—that she's forgotten to telephone someone. Or that she's lost something of importance. She shakes her head again. A friend who does Yoga once insisted it was possible, with a vigorous shake of the head, to rid oneself of bad thoughts. Paige doesn't believe it but she does it anyway. She intones silently: Let it go, let it go, let it go.

She blows her nose. Crumpled up tissues, the day's detritus, are strewn about the room. In a drawer, the second drawer in her dresser, the dresser she inherited from her grandmother, there are handkerchiefs with "Paige" embroidered on them. She likes to blow her nose into linen handkerchiefs, especially those bearing her name. She runs to the dresser and does just that. She laughs out loud. She feels unwell. Then she telephones a friend but there is no comfort, no release. Her friend says she can barely hear Paige, and why doesn't she see a doctor? They say goodbye. Paige's throat aches. She sits down at her desk.

Words plague her and push through her body, brazenly, hazardously, forced by the breath, the break of life. Her lungs work furiously, her heart beats rapidly in a kind of rhythm, a pulse beat: I love you, I love you, I do. I'm thinking of you all the time. Can you hear my heart beat? It's a furious melody, it's a cacophony, this insistent incessant crazy love I have for you. You're always near. You never go away. Paige thinks she's going to scream. She might not be able to restrain herself. But can she scream? Does she have it in her? If she screams, the neighbors might think she was being murdered.

"A scream ripped from her, tearing the air, renting it as if it were silk. A scream—in the middle of the night, in the middle of a party. Everyone sat there, their hands shaped like cups and saucers. They were indifferent to her, preening. It was not unusual for people to watch themselves in mirrors and admire their images. Oddly enough those people who looked longest were considered the most beautiful. The scream, everyone said, meant nothing.

"She was not without charm. Silky hair fell in waves about her face, covering one of her clever eyes. She clasped her pale hands, crossed her long legs, held herself erect. She lowered her gaze, embarrassed and yet oddly proud. He danced toward her, embraced her and then regaled her with stories of places she had never been. After this she did a slight dance that went unobserved by everyone but the tea drinker. The tea drinker gestured, beckoning with compassion. She caught the look but acknowledged it a little too seriously. Both grew uncomfortable.

"In the corner, too close to her, was a man who repeated himself endlessly. He had a square jaw. She listened to him and could not listen to him. He spoke in a monotone but even so he was sometimes perceptive and entertaining, in a tragic sort of way. They had once been lovers for reasons she could not fully remember. And one day, suddenly, she no longer wanted him to penetrate her. The very thought of making love with him became abhorrent to her. He could not understand her reluctance to engage in an act they had done many times before. But then he repeated himself endlessly, so how should he understand?

"Her brothers strode into the room. The sight of them caused her a simultaneity of pain and pleasure. She was speechless. She wished they would leave. An old feeling, a dusty antique gown, wrapped her in perpetual childhood."

She feared she must stay there always. She wanted to believe something else. The room enclosed her. She could not breathe. She was a fish out of water. She was an uninvited guest. A stranger, a madwoman, a whore. She was an explorer who didn't like what she found. She swooned. She screamed.

"The scream came from someone she did not know, as if a lodger had taken a room in her without her consent. The scream was unpleasant, though not completely unmusical. It was pitched high, at the top of a tall tree, at the top of a winter tree, bare of leaves, stark against a steel-grey sky. Naked branches, fingers pointing to the abyssal sky, would scream the way she did if they could."

The words lie there and they may be lies. They lie on the page. They are little worms. Once she dreamed, on the night before a reading she was to give, that rather than words on paper, there were tiny objects linked one to another, which she had to decipher instantly and turn into words, sentences, a story, flawlessly, of course. Funny fear of the blank page. Didn't she recently explain that writing was erasure, because the words were already there, already in the world, that the page wasn't blank.

In the room there is no sound other than her own breathing and the rattle of the windows. An eerie sound. The wind is blowing hard against them. The windows may shatter. Their rattling is like a wheeze from a dying person. A death rattle, a wail. The buffeted windows emit a sad human sound. Paige is sensitive to sound, the way some people are sensitive to smell. Her mother was an opera singer, a soprano who quit midcareer to marry Paige's father. Sometimes her mother would sing when she did housework. When Paige was little she disliked her mother's voice. Later she admired it.

Paige doesn't like the sound of her own voice. When she has laryngitis, her voice settles deep in her throat and sounds raspy.

Call it sexy. Do you think so? Perhaps the voice intimates a
threatening possibility. It may be saying: I come from down here.
I am in your body. I am, like you, from an animal. I growl. I am
covered by soft hair. I go out of control, I like to be touched, and
were you to reach inside me and find that hidden place, it would
surprise you. It would terrify you. The urgency is raw and harsh,
like this voice that has been taken away, taken by the wind or
gods or ancestors. When I cannot talk at all, will you listen to me?

"It is the night of the world. Life is dark and hidden from me.
The animals cannot sleep. The mountains are complacent and
stalwart. The caves are shy, without light. The plains don't want
to be flat. The desert is listless, waiting. I have been sitting here
a very long time listening to the wind as it races past. It is howling
and wailing, it is crying. It pules. It shakes the glass in the
windowpanes. I stare out into the dark night. I am completely
alone, my hand caresses my neck. The beauty of the world
stretches away from me."

Page pats her left shoulder absentmindedly. She strokes her neck.
She has a long thin neck upon which her head balances precari-
ously, like an exotic bird's might, a salmon pink bird that can be
found only in a hot southern clime. Paige has never been to the
tropics. It is cold in the room. Her throat is sore. It hurts like a
broken window.

"Where does the wind rush and why does it gallop away? How
to describe the fascinating horror of natural forces, to describe

the body of the world which envelops me and exists outside my body? The house is old. It is old enough to be an antique. The shadows in the room obscure the objects in it. I sit on a chair made of dark wood. I am wearing blue cotton pajamas that my father once wore. Blue is the color of hope. I nursed my father for many years before his death. He died of throat cancer. At the end he could not speak. I have my memories. They are fixed and still like his dead body. It is almost morning but the sun has not yet completely risen."

The effect wasn't what she wanted. Paige probably ought to weave these paragraphs into the scream story. It might work. It might fit. It might be fitting but she cannot decide. She is lost at sea and cast in doubt. She is scrambling for words and glances helplessly at her books. Her guard is down. Right now, were you to criticize her or, worse, insult her, she'd be stunned, crushed. Look: She crumples before your sharp eyes, her face falls, actually falls, as if the bones that construct it and the skin that the bones support had given up, given her up, given up on her. Crestfallen, she is as helpless as an animal that has had the misfortune to be shot with a tranquillizer dart.

Have you ever seen an elephant go down when injected with such a drug? A sorry sight. The elephant drops like a sack of concrete; it falls like a building exploded by dynamite. One can watch it happen in nature films, which Paige likes very much. Animals move her in a way that human beings never do. She will not admit this nor will she write about it. Her parents gave away her dog. She didn't talk for weeks. Her calico cat ate her powder blue parakeet. The cat was given away. She was beyond words and didn't even write about it in her diary. Her father asked: Cat got your tongue, Paige?

"It is in the unconscious that fantasy, moments of the day, and memory live, a reservoir for the poetry of the world. Is everything else prose? Is what's conscious ordinary prose, the prose of the world?"

Or, I tease, the pose of the world. She is separating much too neatly the world she knows—I nearly wrote word for world—from the world she doesn't know, the one that owns her and to which she is a slave. She is a slave to what she can't remember and doesn't know and she is a slave to what she remembers and what she thinks she knows. Her education has damaged her in ways she does not even know.

Paige suffers mainly from reminiscences. Memories come in floods, in half-heard phrases, in blurry snapshots. They merge into one another. They have no edges. They emerge in the mountains, in movie theaters, in fields, on the road; they erupt in rooms, in cafes, when she walks, they come all the time. They come when she is talking to friends. They come and her friends disappear in front of her as she fights to clarify a faded image, reassemble a dubious moment, inhale a familiar scent.

Impossible past, what did that perfume smell like, what did his voice sound like, where does the air linger so sweetly, where did her train set go, where was the playground, who are the small people playing funny, frightening games, who called her name. What is whispering? She is captive to impossibility. She opens her notebook, then turns on the radio. An advertisement asks: "Would you like to speak French? It's easier than you think." On the news a missile is referred to as a "technological hero." She turns off the radio. She chooses music from many cassettes which are piled one on top of the other. Her hand covers her mouth, an old gesture, and she coughs; then her index finger slides free and touches her top lip. She looks as if she is musing, being her own muse.

One of Paige's favorite songs, "I'm Your Puppet," was recorded by James and Bobby Purify. It was popular years ago, but she didn't know when it was written, and maybe the Purifys—purify, could that really have been their name?—maybe they were no longer alive. No matter when she heard the song, morning or night, and no matter where she was, she always felt what she felt when she heard the song for the first time. Paige can even remember where she was and with whom: near her high school, in a fast-food joint, with a rock and roll musician; and she even remembers what he said to her about the song—he was curious why she liked it so much, wasn't she perverse? She remembers how she felt when the tune ended and also when the relationship ended, curiously and insignificantly.

Pull a string and I'll wink at you
I'm your puppet
I'll do funny things if you want me to
I'm your puppet

I'm yours to have and to hold
Darling, you've got full control
Of your puppet . . .

Paige is dancing in front of the mirror. She is moving her hips. She is swaying, her eyes are closed, she is traveling, she is faraway. Sinuous motion. She is everywhere and nowhere.

Just pull them little strings
And I'll sing you a song
Make me do right or make me do wrong
I'm your puppet.

After she listened to it over and over, she wondered if the Purifys actually felt like puppets, and then she wondered why she cared. It was a song they sang. They didn't write it. Maybe they hated singing it. Maybe they didn't like the melody. Maybe they hated the words. Paige can give you the lyrics, not the tune. Do you know the song and do you hear it when you read the words?

Paige knew a woman, just a girl really, who had memorized practically every song that had ever been written, and she could play and sing beautifully. They met in Berlin, on a summer day, as the Wall came down. The girl had a guitar strapped to her back. Paige swallows hard and remembers Agnes. Agnes is a lump in her throat.

"Agnes was tall—oh Agnes, agony—so tall, she could have played pro basketball if she were a man, and she was built like one, bearing broad shoulders and a heavy jaw. Instead she played the guitar in a militant way typical of those still influenced by Dylan and Odetta. She played when she begged on the street, near the subway at Astor Place, which is where I usually found her, standing not far from a woman in her fifties who did small paintings she sold for a dollar, usually religious themes in a wild style. I bought many, for a dollar, a bargain, and gave them to friends, and some knew they were worth something, that there was a special kind of mind at work in those small paintings, with their vivid blues and muted greens. She might use as background a lime yellow and dot some rose on it, the rose was a rose; or the theme was religious, something like nuns talking on telephones, as if in direct communication with god.

"Agnes ignored the painter. Agnes didn't like art, it didn't seem to her to serve the purpose music and words did, didn't speak to her, and she was deeply involved in speaking. Agnes talked all the time or sang all the time. She tended to shout the later at night it was, the closer it came to the time when she should have gone home if she had had a home, which she didn't. She stayed with me once, but only once, because she wanted to talk all night about music and writing. I wanted to watch *Hill Street Blues* or something soothing: the captain of the precinct and his wife the lawyer end up in bed, to love away their troubles or to discuss stoically their harrowing day, one filled with more catastrophe than anyone else's. Except maybe Agnes'. I like to be in bed when people on television are in bed. But not Agnes, she didn't want to sleep and could talk all night and I don't know when she slept. She could talk endlessly. I think she liked the sound of her own voice.

"Agnes was unattractive. Her lumbering awkwardness seemed to come from her difficulty in just being alive, of her being acutely aware of her bulky frame and plain face. She must have conceived of herself as a burden to behold. She walked with her head down. She stooped over, bending herself to the ground to make her big body less significant or impressive, less noticeable. Tall people stoop over which is why they often have bad backs. I read that in a book I proofed about back pain—I work as a proofreader—I'd never thought about back pain before and after I finished it, having read that it can happen at any time, out of the blue, that you can turn your head, or pick up a cup, and boom, your back goes out and you're in pain for weeks, there was something else to worry about, something else to be anxious about that could happen to you seemingly at random. But can anything that happens in your body be at random? I told Agnes to stand up straight but she wouldn't listen and I'm sure she'll be a stooped old woman if she lives that long. But where is Agnes? Did she go back to Minnesota? Will I hear that voice of hers again?

"Agnes pretends not to suffer. That's her glory. She depresses me but then I'm not able to suffer happily the way she does. Agnes is the most Christian person I know. She doesn't hate anyone and carries her belongings around with her as if nomadism were her chosen lot in life, not simply a sign of her poverty. Most every day I'd see her and sometimes I'd take her for a coffee or a bowl of soup at a diner. She was remarkably presentable and never smelled. I have to admit that if she did I wouldn't have been able to go around with her. It's gotten so I can't walk into some restaurants because of the stench of cockroach spray. It suffocates me. I move away from people who have bad breath. What's happening in their bodies, I wonder. I don't know where Agnes bathed or showered but she kept herself clean. She had her secrets and lived in a secret way. I don't know what's happened to her though, she's not around, and it's so cold out. Will I ever hear her sing again? Her voice cut into the night like a knife."

Cut to: Interior—a studio apartment in Manhattan. It is raining. Paige is sleeping. She awakens and begins to cough. She has no voice. She remembers her dream. In it she is making love with a man. He wants her desperately, the passion is incredible, huge, overpowering, bigger than both of them. But he is impotent. They stop. They start again. He cannot. His flesh is weak. Then he crawls into her arms and lies across her lap. They form the Pietà. In the dream she says to him, So you would rather be the baby than the penis.

In another dream her father is alive. He speaks to her. Then he dies in front of her, as he always does in her dreams. She comforts her mother, in the dream, by saying, At least I was able to hear his voice again.

"Cut to: A woman at her desk, writing her dreams furiously. She is laughing, she is crying. She tears one sheet of paper out of the typewriter, then another, and another, and after several hours of intense work, she has a pile of papers in front of her. Victoriously she prints the 'End' at the bottom of the last page."

How Paige wishes her life were scripted. how she wishes for inspiration, though she does not find it and doesn't believe in it. Must one believe? How she wishes she did. If wishes were horses . . .

> Pull another string and I'll kiss your lips
> Snap your fingers and I'll turn you some tricks
> I'm your puppet
> Your every wish is my command
> All you gotta do is wiggle your hand
> I'm your puppet.

If Paige continues and even finishes the Agnes story she might title it *Ordinary Unhappiness*. Though maybe Agnes' was neurotic unhappiness. Maybe it ought to be called *Dramatic Pictures*. Dramatic Agnes wasn't easy to forget. She lingered in Paige's mind, in the air, as vaporous memory. You might say Agnes was unique. You might say she was pathetic. Wounded certainly, a wounded baby animal. Paige hears Agnes' clear voice as if she were singing in the room, beside her. Then inside her. Agnes' voice quivers in Paige, strikes a knowing chord, hits a funny bone.

Surely you know people like Agnes. Their voices are sheltered in your body. They have become phrases in your body. They are your visitors. Sometimes you push them away, push them out, exhale them heavily. You don't want them inside you. You may want to kill them. I don't want them either. I am too full and too empty. The bombs are falling. People are maimed, dead. I can barely think, let alone speak. What should I do? I must offer you something. I must prove something. I have something to prove. I will prove it to you. Words will be transformed into wishes.

Paige is holding her head in her hands. Noises from the street disturb her, urge her from her chair. She rushes to the open window. The neighbors, Debbie and Ricky are fighting again. They are screaming, their faces ugly, their bodies twisted, distorted by fury and drugs.

"Back home, Jesus says to me, 'Debbie likes to get hit, man, she's sick. Ricky tells her to stop yelling and then slaps her and she goes, More, more, hit me again.' I don't know whether or not to believe Jesus. I don't want to. But I've never known him to lie. He asked me once, 'Are you going to write about my family? It'd make a bestseller, it's a horror story. Everybody'd want to read it. They'd make a movie about it. You'd make millions.'

"Jesus plays basketball with the guys who hang out across the street. Some come from other neighborhoods. Jesus is the only one of his family who's made friends on the block. He's open, gentle. Ricky used to beat him up. Ricky's beat him up since he was a little boy. Now Jesus is bigger than Ricky. Last week he bashed Ricky's head against a wall. He tells me, 'Ricky won't try nothing ever again.' These days Ricky's on crack, not smack, so at least he's not dropping syringes out the window into the backyard, which was upsetting, watching needles fall on the garden.

"I wasn't sure if I were seeing slides or a film of the scene, it all happened so fast before my eyes. First Debbie ran forward and showed me the scars on her arms. That was awful. Then she tells me that her baby Jessica is one year old. She shows me Jessica's picture. Jessica is in Debbie's arms. The image is fuzzy and dark. Debbie's in pink and the child is looking up at her, smiling at her. I think it's a smile. Showing me the picture, Debbie is happy, as if the baby had not been taken away from her."

So many stories. So many voices. All in need. In need of comfort. I am your comfort. I hold you. I let you go. I am true to you. I am a secret. I explain everything. I seduce you. You lose yourself. I am what you have lost. Your elusive past. Your fleeting present. Your irresistible and horrifying future. I am the little things in life. And the big things. I am lyrical. I am logical. I am steady. I am faithless. I am prosaic. I am poetic. I am hard. I am tender. I am the voice of reason. Of sanity. Of history. I will sing you an aria.

"No. I said no. And I said no again, and I said again, No, no, and I whispered No, and I sang No, and I screamed No, and then I said No, again, and again, and then I yelled No, never more, no, and no, and I hissed, No, then called out, No, then I murmured quietly, No, never, not again, no, and then, with more voice, shouted, No. No. No. No. Never. Never."

I find it difficult to separate the beginning from the end, which makes it hard to record stories, to invent them, or erase them. This may be the end for Paige but stories go on and on and on, leading one into another relentlessly. There is no end to stories, they are without mercy. Still, you and I know stories that begin and end, as surely as you and I know that death comes to all things.

"We do not select the stories we write, we do not pick the voices. They take us by surprise and we surrender to them. They write us, they write in us, all over us, all through us. They occupy us. We are, in a sense, puppets—to language, with language."

Not truly, not absolutely, not actually, not completely.

    The night draws to a close, but it doesn't draw. The day dawns, but not for Paige. She is asleep, a small creature curled into the corner of her bed. She covers her head with a blanket. She burrows deeper into her dream. She dreams she has something wonderful to say and then she wakes up, and begins her day, first stopping the alarm clock, then making a cup of coffee, then looking for a shirt, then sitting at her desk. To find words. Paige wraps her hand around her neck and rubs her throat. She coughs and coughs.

Lynne Tillman

TV TALES

Your frenzied
dictations. Your
control-freak
vigilance. Your
selective memory.

Think like us

Within the image:
Your frenzied
dictations. Your
control-freak
vigilance. Your
selective memory.

Think like us

Barbara Kruger, Untitled (Think Like Us), *1994.*
Photograph. Courtesy of the artist

TV TALES

There was a man who loved his dog. The dog was as loyal as the day was long. But the man had a hard life. The only good thing in it was his dog. So he threw himself off the lower level of the Queensboro Bridge, into the East River. He held his dog in his arms. The dog was discovered in the river, tugging at the man's body. He was trying to carry his master to shore. But the man was dead, and the dog was placed in a shelter.

There was a little girl. She wanted to be a movie star. She plotted and worked hard. She became a star, universally adored. But she was vain and insecure, and as the years went by, she became more and more afraid of the public who loved her. She labored for hours to achieve the right look, but as she got older it took more and more time. Finally she spent all her time preparing her face. She never left the house. Her fans forgot her, and she committed suicide.

There was a violent man. He bludgeoned, skinned and butchered a neighbor's pit bull-collie mutt. Then he barbecued the meat on a home gas grill. The dog's head was found on a fence outside the neighbor's house. The violent man was sent to jail. The lawyer said of his client, "When he gets to state prison, and he's the only one there on an offense like this one, I don't think it's going to do him a bit of good."

There was an unfriendly old woman. She worked all her life and then she retired. She never said hello to anyone. When she stopped leaving her house, and her neighbors never saw her at all, they mowed her unruly lawn and collected her mail. Then, one day, when her house was falling apart and the stink became unbearable, the neighbors called the cops. They discovered that the unfriendly old woman been dead for four years. The telephone was near her rotting body. A neighbor said, "No one's to blame. She never said hello to anyone."

There was a man whose wife left him. They had four children. He didn't want a divorce, but she did. He tried to get her back and pleaded, but she said no, never. And she expected him to help support their kids. He became more and more enraged and frustrated. So he phoned her one day and arranged to take the whole family for a drive. He planted a bomb in his car and picked them up. The bomb exploded. He killed them and himself with one blast. "HE WAS EVIL," a headline screamed. "Love rage drove dad to blow up his family."

There was an unhappy husband. He watched TV all night. His wife was bored with him and complained. He just wanted to be left alone and dreamed about running away or murdering her. But he couldn't do it. His wife wanted to divorce him, but she couldn't do it. She hated her job, too. Her boss yelled at her, and she yelled at her husband. They were stuck with each other. He sulked in front of the TV every night. She drank. At fifty-five he died of a heart attack. He left all his money to charity. His wife couldn't break his will and had to take another job to support herself. She couldn't control her temper and lost both jobs. She ended her life on welfare and blamed him for everything.

There was a woman who wanted to be skinny. She ate no fat or starch. She kept no food in her house. Her eyes grew big in her head. She stared hungrily at friends as they ate their food. One day she disappeared. It's said she wasted away.

There was a happy couple. They couldn't live without each other. They were never apart. They were everything to each other. If you were friends with one, you were friends with the other. If you saw one, you saw the other. You made a date with one, there was the other. At dinner they ordered for each other. Occasionally one of them would complain about the other. But that was rare and unimportant. They were everything to each other. They were never apart. They couldn't live without each other. They died on the same day.

There was a determined wife who stayed home and took care of the children. But her husband was cheap. He didn't give her enough household money. She argued with him and grew to hate him. One day she met a young man and fell in love. For a while she was furtively happy. Then she and her lover went to a hitman and arranged to have her husband murdered, for $10,000. She saved her meager household allowance. Her husband also fell in love with someone else and went to the same hitman to murder his wife. Both plots were foiled, and the miserable pair went to jail.

There was a woman whose only wish was to be beautiful. But when she looked into the mirror, she saw only flaws. Her friends told her she was crazy, so she didn't trust her friends. The truth was her mirror. She went to a plastic surgeon. He changed every feature on her face. She didn't look like the woman she once was and liked herself better. She made new friends. Then one day she found fault with her new face. She moved to another part of the country, had more surgery and made other friends. She wasn't satisfied, though, and kept having surgery. Eventually her nose was smaller than her lips, and she couldn't breathe. So she expired.

There was a woman who wanted a child. The man she was with didn't know if he did. He said he loved her so much, he wanted her all to himself. She waited a long time for him to agree. And when finally he did, she hated him. So she left him and never had a child.

There was a young woman who liked to drink blood. She met a man who had advertised his "wish to become a donor to a female vampire." It was love at first bite. Now they nibble and suck each other's necks, happily. They trust each other to be forever free of disease and think they're ageless. "Drinking blood's very intimate," the young woman says. "Also I like pain to a certain degree."

There was a woman whose lover was unhappy. He always wanted to commit suicide. But she loved him very much, and, no matter what, she wanted his baby. Every time he failed to kill himself, she'd accompany him the day after to a sperm bank where he'd make a deposit. Finally he succeeded, and his suicide note read: "I would rather take my own life now than be ground into a mediocre existence by my enemies." He left behind fifteen vials of sperm, which he bequeathed to the woman. But his former spouse and their children objected to the woman's having artificial insemination after his suicide. So the battle raged in court, which lately sided with the woman and decreed that sperm was property and could be passed on. The decision's being appealed. Meanwhile, the woman visits the Cyrobank and speaks to the vials. "Hang on there," she says to the sperm, "you'll be here soon."

There was a young woman who worked her way up the ladder. Many people in her company envied her, but she had her boss' approval. Then one day her boss died, and she was fired.

There was a married couple who were very much in love. But one day the man saw his beloved talking to the mailman. He became enraged and slapped his wife. He told her not to leave the house or talk to anyone. The woman was afraid and stayed home. But finally one day the terrified woman ran away. She left the house and him for good. But her husband followed her and menaced her. The wife went to court to obtain a protection order against him. So the husband murdered her in the courthouse.

There were two brothers. They had a strict mother. She was religious and made them study hard. The older brother hated her. He wanted to kill her. He asked his younger brother to help him. He was going to use a crossbow and arrow. The brothers argued. The younger one refused to do it. So the older brother shot him with the crossbow and arrow. The arrow lodged in his neck, but he survived. "He did get seriously injured," said a detective, "but he had God with him." Their forgiving mother expressed no vengeful feelings toward her older son. The mother was just "trying to cope with the tragedy of having one son in the hospital and the other in custody," the police said.

There was an ordinary woman. The woman had a dream. In it, someone wrote a book about her. The ordinary woman read the book and exclaimed, "There's nobody like me."

There was a sweet little girl. When her mother loved her, she thought her daughter was good enough to eat. When her mother hated her, she thought her daughter was the devil. One day, at the school cafeteria where she worked, the mother placed the little girl in the oven. She set the temperature to 425 degrees. School employees quickly removed the girl. But the girl went to the hospital with second-degree burns all over her body.

There was a man who loved cookies. He couldn't control himself around them. He was an overweight bumbler and hapless burglar. His wife left him after he was released from his second stint in the slammer. He became very depressed. He broke into a restaurant. He wanted to steal the safe, but he tripped the burglar alarm. He grabbed four chocolate chip cookies and fled. He was caught, cookie-handed. It was his third felony, a third strike for him under the new three-strikes-and-you're-out California law. So he was sentenced to twenty-six years in jail. "That's six and a half years per cookie," said his public defender.

There was a German tourist in Florida. He was on a plane back to Germany. It was about to take off, but he had to piss very badly. He didn't speak much English. He called the attendant over and used German slang, which he translated into English. He said, "Then the roof flies." They thought he was a terrorist, and was threatening to bomb the plane, so they put him in jail for nine months. At his hearing the judge said, "Do you see anything that happened that couldn't have been remedied by letting this man go to the bathroom?"

There was a moderately autistic boy. He was lost for four days in a snake-filled swamp. Somehow he survived. When asked about his time alone in the dark and cold, he said, "I see fish, lots of fish." His mother had always encouraged him to enjoy a life as close to normal as possible. The boy had learned to swim, and he swam like a dolphin. It was probably how he endured a desperate situation that four Rangers hadn't—they all died of hypothermia. The boy's mother, Mrs. Touchstone, thought lightning might've "penetrated his shell" and kept her son swimming, moving. "Do you really think," Mrs. Touchstone asked, "God would strike him dead with lightning? Wouldn't that be redundant?"

LYNNE TILLMAN

Both images: Jane Dickson, from LIVING WITH
CONTRADICTIONS, *1980. Monoprint on rice paper.
9¹/₂ x 7¹/₂ inches. Courtesy of the artist.*

LIVING WITH CONTRADICTIONS

He didn't want to fight in any war and she didn't want to have a child. They had been living together for three years and still didn't have a way to refer to each other that didn't sound stupid, false, or antiquated. Language follows change and there wasn't any language to use.

Partners in a pair bonded situation; that sounded neutral. Of course living with someone isn't a neutral situation. Julie and Joe aren't cave dwellers. They don't live together as lovers or as husband and wife.

How long would this century be called modern or, even, post-modern? Perhaps relationships between people in the 14th century were more equitable, less fantastic. Not that Julie would've wanted to have been the miller's wife, or Joe, the miller.

In other centuries, different relationships. Less presumption, less intimacy? Before capitalism, early capitalism, no capitalism, feudalism. Feudal relationships. I want one of those, Julie thought, something feudal. What would it be like not to have a contemporary mind?

Intimacy is something people used to talk about before commercials. Now there's nothing to say.

People are intimate with their analysts, if they're lucky. What could be more intimate than an advertisement for Ivory soap? It's impossible not to be affected.

The manufacture of desire and the evidence of real desire. But "real" desire is for what—for what is real or manufactured?

Other people's passions always leave you cold. There is nothing like really being held. They didn't expect to be everything to each other.

The first year they lived together was a battle to be together and to be separate. A silent battle, because you can't fight and fight together, it defeats the purpose of the battle.

You can't talk about relationships, at least they didn't; they talked about things that happened and things that didn't. Daily life is very daily.

The great adventure, the pioneering thing, is to live together and not be a couple. The expectation is indefatigable and exhausting. Julie bought an Italian postcard, circa 1953, showing an ardent man and woman, locked in embrace. And looking at each other. Except that one of her eyes was roving out, the other in, and his eyes, looking at her, were crossed.

Like star-crossed lovers' eyes should be, she thought. She drew a triangle around their eyes, which made them still more distorted. People would ask "Where's Joe?" as if there was something supposed to be attached to her. The attachment, my dear, isn't tangible, she wanted to say, but it is also physical.

New cars, new lovers. Sometimes she felt like Ma Kettle in a situation comedy, looked on from outside. You're either on the inside looking out or the outside looking in. (Then there's the inside looking in, the outside looking out.)

Joe: We're old love.

Julie: We're familiar with each other.

Julie didn't mind except that she didn't have anyone new to talk about, the way her friends did. Consumerism in love. One friend told her that talking about the person you lived with was like airing your clean laundry in public.

Familiarity was, for her, better than romance. She'd been in love enough. Being in love is a fiction that lasts an hour and a half, feature-length, and then you're hungry again. Unromantic old love comforted her, like a room to read in.

Joe: You hooked up with me at the end of your hard-guy period.

Julie: How do you know?

Joe: I know.

So, Julie and Joe were just part of the great heterosexual, capitalist family thrall, possessing each other.

Contradictions make life finer. Ambivalence is just another word for love, becoming romantic about the unconscious.

Where does one find comfort, even constancy. To find it in an idea or in the flesh. We do incorporate ideas, after all.

You can accept the irrational over and again, you can renounce your feelings every day, but you're still a baby. An infant outside of reason, speaking reasonably about the unreasonable.

Calling love desire doesn't change the need. Julie couldn't abandon her desire for love. It was a pleasurable contradiction and it was against all reason.

madame realism a fairy tale

Silvia Kolbowski, ENLARGED FROM THE CATALOGUE: THE UNITED STATES OF AMERICA, *1988. View of catalogue component. Silkscreen, printed matter, wood, plexiglass. Collection of the artist. Courtesy of American Fine Arts.*

MADAME REALISM: A FAIRY TALE

"It makes letters! It makes words!" Bruno whispered, as he clung, half-frightened, to Sylvie. "Only I ca'n't make them out! Read them, Sylvie!"

"I'll try," Sylvie gravely replied. "Wait a minute—if only I could see that word—"

"I should be very ill!" a discordant voice yelled in our ears. "Were I to swallow this," he said, "I should be very ill!"

—LEWIS CARROLL, *SYLVIE AND BRUNO*

I n the winter the days end suddenly and with such ferocious indifference that Madame Realism felt at a loss. Day after short day she was caught short, surprised. I'm still capable of surprise, she told herself. When it's dark, one expects surprises, Madame Realism reflected as she looked out the window.

Anyone could imagine anything. The evening sky covered the ordinary street. Upon a night screen we can project wildly but usually we don't, she reassured herself, most of the time people fill in the spaces with the familiar. Madame Realism closed the curtains and wondered if she had disappeared. Even if she were visible, and viewable, she wouldn't necessarily be any better known. Recognized perhaps, but not known. Madame Realism didn't subscribe to the wisdom that what you see is what you get.

That night, after watching television and reading Lewis Carroll's *Sylvie and Bruno,* Madame Realism couldn't fall asleep. She tossed and turned, much like a ship at sea during a storm, much like a well-used phrase. Finally, exhausted, she fell into a deep, undisturbed sleep. She dreamed that she entered a museum which was a labyrinth. She didn't know what to look for or where to look. She stumbled about, searching for clues. A friend guided her through a cavernous space and pointed out a word or letter from an alphabet Madame Realism didn't know. These shapes appeared on walls and suggested answers. At the end of the dream—do dreams have ends?—Gertrude Stein's deathbed retort to the friend who had asked her, "What is the answer?" flashed on an unfinished wall: "What is the question?"

The next morning Madame Realism awakened slowly, perplexed by the question as an answer. Taken comprehensively, Stein's deathbed statement could require that each day become an investigation, if not an invention. What a struggle, Madame Realism thought, to invent each day. She tried to lift the blankets off her and swing her legs over the side of the bed as she did every morning. But she couldn't move. She could barely open her eyes. It was as if a veil had been placed over them.

"Gradually, however, the conviction came upon me that I could, by a certain concentration of thought, think the veil away. . . ."

After a while Madame Realism was able to pry her eyelids open. And instantly she apprehended a change in herself. It was nothing short of fantastic. Madame Realism was enfolded between stiff cardboard covers, on creamy white paper, stuffed with references and descriptions, and illustrated with photographs, charts and drawings. There were numbers and letters next to some of her paragraphs which referred to artwork that might hang on walls or sit inside plastic boxes on platforms. Madame Realism had turned into a catalogue.

It was frightening and oddly pleasurable. Uncanny. Uncategorizable. But Madame Realism was at home with ambivalence. Her metamorphosis, not that dissimilar from Gregor Samsa's into a cockroach, could be liberating, she told herself as she smoothed her pages and admired her typeface. (She had once been a menu but not for long. The restaurant had closed. It was possible that now she might accompany a permanent installation. She didn't know.)

Ordinarily Madame Realism existed as, or in, a story or essay. No—matter she soothed herself by thinking—I am always fiction. And now, she remarked aloud, reviewing herself, I do not have to pretend to be a tabula rasa, to pretend that I don't have a past, that I don't have a history. She turned herself to another page, imagining that she was "taking a page from this book." She reconsidered: I am a page from this book. As she studied herself

Madame Realism mused, I am a compendium, a list, a detailed enumeration, a register. I can provide a provenance. Haughtily and awkwardly she whirled about and sang: I am a woman with a past, a danger to the community.

"How convenient it would be," Lady Muriel laughingly remarked, "if cups of tea had no weight at all! Then perhaps ladies would sometimes be permitted to carry them for short distances."

Perhaps I'm dreaming, Madame Realism told herself, maybe I haven't actually awakened. Didn't the *Tibetan Book of the Dead* insist that one could not know one was alive? Consequently one might be dead. As if an idea had blown in from the chilly outdoors and seized her, Madame Realism seized upon the notion that she might have become the catalogue to the exhibition she hadn't found in her dream. Her immaterial dream world might have a life of its own. And Madame Realism could merely be the key to it. (She struggled between proposing herself as its analogue or homologue.) It made a strange kind of sense, that she was a catalogue to herself more than to anything else, and to her unconscious rather than the other way around. What she perceived and apprehended was necessarily and always in some way constitutive of herself. This wasn't exactly reassuring. But Madame Realism expected to view herself with alarm. She suspected some would grow complacent in her place.

In this new guise, Madame Realism could be a Beatrice or Virgil to any Dante in need of Faith or Reason. She was meant to enlighten and educate. She could be taken off the shelf, opened up, browsed through and absorbed; she could become well thumbed and might even become well regarded. Madame

Realism pushed aside some of her words, set in Times Roman, to enter in spidery marks traces of her enduring skepticism. How seriously should she be taken? It was hard to think, as she had already been thought.

"That's just what Sylvie says," Bruno rejoined. "She says I wo'n't learn my lessons. And I tells her, over and over, I ca'n't learn 'em. And what do you think she says? She says 'It isn't ca'n't, it's wo'n't!'"

Focus, Madame Realism demanded of herself, concentrate. She couldn't find her reading glasses. Sometimes she misplaced things just to be able to find them again. She spent a certain amount of time every day searching for what she knew was there. Yet relief always arrived at the end of her search—her glasses, book, bag were precisely where she had left them. Still it bored her, going over and over the same territory. Perhaps I am looking for something else, she theorized, and by misplacing things I am actually displacing things, displacing what I think I know, the familiar. The way art does. She wrote invisibly in her margin: If art has a purpose, is it to point to the absence of invention?

But now she was a museum catalogue and the very territory she went over and over was her. In this form she would always be "something that couldn't find its glasses." To others this would be a necessary part of Madame Realism's constitution. Where was her ambiguity to reside? Between her lines, or in her margins, which some might not even notice? To some, margins were nothing more than a frame for the center.

"One needn't be a Doctor," I said, "to take an interest in medical books. There's another class of readers, who are yet more deeply interested—" "You mean the Patients?" she interrupted.

She couldn't get her own measure; it was a matter of scale. From one point of view, she was small. From another, she was big. I am insignificant as well as important. Like Saint Peter, she was the rock upon which the Church was built, she was also ephemera. Many would throw her out. Some would save her. She could no longer adequately describe herself. She had been put in her place and had been transformed into a place. As a reference she was undeniably self-referential.

Madame Realism was puzzled (probably she was a puzzle). As she fretted, she knew her pages would become frayed. That, too, she feared, would be part of her forever. But she didn't know. There were so many things she didn't know and which remained incomprehensible to her. Even as a guide to herself, if that's what she was, she couldn't offer certainty. She could only suspend comprehension long enough to allow questions to rise to the surface, like cream on milk. For instance, was she a source or a resource?

At this Madame Realism's paragraphs shifted. Précis, dates, places and names jiggled about as if an acrobat were upsetting and resetting her type and throwing it into the air. Her pages fell out of order, and like Humpty Dumpty she didn't know whether she'd ever get back together again. It dawned on Madame Realism—in fact it was impressed on her that explanations were as complex as what they were meant to explain. Elementary, my dear Madame Realism, she exclaimed, laughing. She became optimistic. She could overflow with questions. She could be difficult. She could be not easy to follow. She could appear to be transparent and turn out to be opaque. She could even admit her influences—Lewis Carroll, for one. No one would doubt she was a construction. The exhibition in her dream—the art—could be herself. Wasn't she sometimes given to exhibitionism?

"So, either I've been dreaming about Sylvie," I said to myself, "and this is the reality. Or else I've really been with Sylvie, and this is a dream! Is Life itself a dream, I wonder?"

Dreams are wishes, dreams are wishes. This must be a wish, Madame Realism realized as she woke again. Was this the beginning of a new day, one she had to invent? I must want to be an ordinary catalogue. Part of me must have desires in that direction. I want to be cited, to be secure, helpful and clear. Yet I also don't want to be, since I am a continuation of many ideas including, what is the question? who asks? where is it? who decides? am I it? Madame Realism leaped out of bed.

Though alone in her apartment, with just the sound of steam rising through the pipes and radiators, Madame Realism glanced over her shoulder. Would History, or Fate, be standing there, ready to shake her to her very foundations? She felt weighed down by the past and the present. Madame Realism wished she could rise above her concerns, but more and more she knew she was her concerns. She didn't want to be buried beneath her own inchoate and unachievable hopes, like the desire for immortality. It was probably there, though, embarrassed and absurd, mocked and made irrelevant by death.

No longer a catalogue, if she had ever been one, Madame Realism walked to the window and opened the curtain. The sun was shining. She really wasn't sure what she was anymore. She hoped others would have a few ideas. To some extent, a work or text relied on the intelligence, the kindness, of strangers. Madame Realism smiled to herself and stared out the window. She was transfixed by the street's plenty, its wonderful ordinariness.

"Ah, well!" the Gardener said with a kind of groan. "Things change so, here. Whenever I look again it's sure to be something else."

PHANTOMS

LYNNE TILLMAN

Laura Letinsky, UNTITLED, *1995. Chromogenic print. Collection of the artist. Courtesy of Edwynn Houk Gallery.*

PHANTOMS

'm in a house with many rooms, and, like an old joke, I could have a headache in any one of them. Familiar things look unfamiliar; they're not my familiar. This should make my time here exciting, but I'm not excited. I'm nauseated. I don't know any of the people who own or rent the rooms. I'm told I'm related to them.

I carry an album that I inherited, and they could be in it, or I might slot them in, later. I sneak around, relishing scenes. I'm used to sneaking. Many times I've been nearly invisible, and sometimes I've been camouflaged effectively. But I have a powerful curiosity that threatens to blow my cover. My mother taught me that curiosity is everything. But people decide I'm nosy when I ask too many questions. I'm driven, though, and I think they're immune to me, anyway.

   It appears to be safe to look around, which is a judgment call, but then everything must be. Still, implausibly, I make myself scarcer. I align my frame with a doorframe and peer into a room. I see a woman, standing. I perceive her, since she's caught somewhere between here and nothing, in desolate terrain. But she's not alone. A man lies on the bed. She could be feeling sympathy or lust for him; if this were a mystery, she might have poisoned him. Everyone thinks they're being poisoned these days, and maybe they are. I don't know what she's thinking about; that's never available.

> To her, life ricocheted between permanence and obviousness, the remarkable and the unattainable. She defended herself and held the line for fantasy. She'd wanted a man in her bed who loved her. But desire achieved often loses its imagined sweetness. Bitterness rose in her like a wave of resistance. Oh, the thought of it is better.

I assume and presume, then I excuse myself: No, that's not what I meant, no, not that, not at all. I speculate about intimacy. An intimate scene that excludes me might call up a feeling I can't exactly remember having. These are recurring mental pictures, let's say. I walk on.

> A man, a woman. Her uncertainty—is this all there is?— is tendered by a single gesture. She touches his head. He

appreciates her, thinks he loves her, and wants her to stay. He wants her more, because she wants to leave.

I witness and interpret ancient things. It's a dangerous job that everyone does, so no one even acknowledges it. I resemble what I describe—I imitate gestures, too—talk the talk, walk the walk. I wish I didn't see the way I do. I'd like to drop in on unexpected realities, but I can't follow a rigorous diet of change.

Suddenly a man holds up a fist.

Impossible questions shook futilely in him. He wouldn't answer an inner voice if it called him. Anyway, in what language? Bloody, organ diction. If it spoke his language, he'd hear what he wanted to hear. He went inside, which wasn't a place. He was in a blue jacket, smoking. He thought, Romance is a distraction from death, and I'm in her bathrobe.

I kind of like bathrobe humor.

My album is old-fashioned, long playing; it can be replayed as long as I'm here, then shelved for an eternity. Though everyone's dead in it already, in a way, they're eternally undead, which means everlasting if preserved. Life isn't a retrospective, but I've often tried to lead it that way.

My stalwart looking is defiant. I move on. In a splendid room, a man is acting like a clown.

He asks, Is life or art holding up a mirror?

He grips a hand mirror.

A woman looks at herself in it.

I'm dressed even when I'm naked, she says, glancing down at her funny feet. Her toes are coiled expectantly.

Does my voyeurism suit your exhibitionism? he asks.

Oh yes. I love our perverse marriage.

Come here, he says.

I rely upon wild speculation. I'm not just filling in the blanks. I'm surrounded by people all the time. They're everywhere, resonant and reverberating.

He is near her and, breathing deeply, his chest heaves upward. (Can you picture this?) She watches his intake of breath and waits for a similarly intense exhalation. She wonders if she should regulate her breathing, to breathe with him. She ponders this and then starts—in, out, in, out, in, out. She's with him.

He's full of schemes for them, too.

Tell me a romantic story, she says.

He closes his eyes, because her impassive face makes his yearning almost unbearable.

I'm glad we're not still in love, she adds, provocatively.

Pandora opened the box. If she hadn't, there wouldn't be any stories. Mine are never just personal, they're part of a big, continuous party, thrown by everyone, where everyone's talking,

telling tall and short tales. Everyone's invited. Without these rowdy
events and the next day's maskings and unmaskings, things dim
or tarnish and then turn dull. There's no thrill without exposure,
and without light, there's just nothing.

Without wanting, there's nothing, too, as hard as wanting is.
I'm probably hungry for anything. I can't tell until I eat. But what
will nourish me, when so much is insubstantial and unsatisfying.
Fast food has its place, but disappears fast, too. When stock isn't
kept, details vanish in the cupboard. Still, I keep looking. I often
have to make things up. The instances I can recollect, the scenes
that appear again and again, drifting toward me and away, with
remembered smells that are more fragrant and pungent and
inconceivable with time, don't feel how pleasure feels. Or pain.
They don't give me that. Pictures of pleasure and pain anticipate
my own. Or devour it. Phantoms.

He has sex with the wrong women. He only realizes that
later, but he has to, in order to know what he wants. He
wonders about the urge to be inside her. Maybe almost
any woman. He likes this one, though, she's funny, like
his dumb urges, when they didn't destroy him.

He was like a lot of other guys she knew or thought she
knew. She listens to him. He talks for a long time about
his life, his ambitions. She wishes his lips were fuller.
Many men she'd been with barely had lips. She finds
tight-lipped, tight-assed guys, or they find her.

The incompleteness that rueful existence doles out is skewed and accompanied by blocked views. Illusion's a huge piece of the rugged psychological landscape. Some days I embrace the crazy mess it is, like a best friend. Then, carrying the album, whining about the irretrievable past, mourning the passing of friendships to attrition and death, I actually lose a best friend.

Evidence of nostalgia is everywhere.

I rub away its sticky traces. But I'm becoming nostalgic about nostalgia. So I've considered destroying the album. It's not totally mine, though, and it's impossible to get rid of, anyway.

There are habits of seeing, I have them. I haven't yet experienced the ambivalence of amnesia. I want to know how I'll be pictured, if there's any room for me, what my life appears like clothed in all its anxious, comic, tired, and excited costumes, to me and others. If I had that collection, I might lose interest in others. Or I'd look at it, then realize I wanted something else.

I run up and down the stairs. It's good exercise.

Some rooms are enticing. I want to enter them. But I don't know why they're better, more attractive to me. Taste is a dirty word, and life's my peep show.

Now when I see people embracing, I wonder what they're holding, aside from each other.

Maybe she's thinking: I want you, but I don't want to be in the same situation all the time, and I don't want to settle. I'm young. I see a guy on the street or in a bar, and I think, he's cool, I want him, that. It's the excitement I had with you at the beginning, and I want that.

Maybe he's thinking: When I didn't come through for you the way you thought I should, you said I betrayed you, but you were wrong, because there was nothing I could do. I can't be expected to figure out what the fuck you're thinking if you don't tell me. If women can do that, great, but I can't. I'm not your daddy or mommy, and I don't want to be. OK?

In an embrace, something may be confirmed, avoided, or resolved. Embraces are rewards and consolations. But things come back, anger settles and thickens behind grief and sadness, resolutions don't hold, and an embrace becomes a memory of being held.

What you and I are up against is a picture of happiness. Of being ourselves together, he told her. She wants to say, I don't have fantasies like that. But instead she says she's going to take a shower.

He thinks she's pretty wonderful, but he can't let himself believe it. If he does, he's tempting fate, tempting the big one to rattle his saber, getting closer to death. Everyone dies.
He might as well smoke, he thinks, and reaches for a cigarette.

She screws up her mouth, the way he hates.

I'm a nihilist, he tells her.

She says, What about hypnosis, honey?

If I hang around long enough, I'll trick myself into believing I know what's happening. The real magic acts are the ones no one notices, or sees, not even the magician. We all do them. I could perform some razzle-dazzle and tell myself: This is just like home. But I don't know where home is now.

Someone's upstairs, pacing heavily. A man is at the front door, waving lackadaisically. He appears to be coming and going.

He's going for the newspaper, it's Sunday, or if it's
Tuesday, he's going for a quart of milk and then he'll split
for work. Maybe he'll make coffee. He needs his coffee.
He always needs it. He's sodden and fat with repetition.
He needs to get away.

Weird how a door is an exit and an entrance, enigmatic as expression. I don't like the word "expression," but others are just as limp. He's the right size for the door. It fits him better than his suit. Mostly I take doors for granted.

Now he's turning toward me. There could be conflict. I don't want to fight. I don't want to relax, either, and I don't want to wait around. I rush out the door, when he's not looking. I'm uneasy. Suddenly something feels really wrong, like a hole has opened up inside me. I may be sick.

But I've only forgotten something. I have to return.

I don't want to leave or misplace anything, but it's inevitable. I hang on to things, because I'm sure I'll want them later, at the end. Then I'll reflect upon the past and come up with some mystifications. I'll draw insufficient conclusions. I've never managed to get the whole human figure on paper. I don't think that's going to change.

PLEASURE ISN'T A PRETTY PICTURE

Lynne Tillman

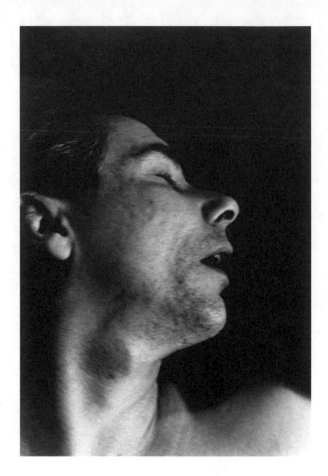

Aura Rosenberg, M.K. 1, 1992. From Headshots.
Gelatin silver print. 16 x 12 inches. Courtesy of
the artist.

PLEASURE ISN'T
A PRETTY PICTURE

When she was fourteen, there was this boy, he was seventeen, he liked girls, sex, she knew it. He was passionate. She could tell just by looking at him. And she knew he meant it, and she knew it was the best thing about him. He wasn't afraid. Mostly what she knew was that he liked it. When she stood near him, she could tell. It drifted off his body, like a smell she could almost recognize.

He looked hard into her when he looked at her. She could feel his intensity, see it in his eyes, in how his eyes didn't leave hers when he looked at her. He was inviting, there was an invitation. Other boys were shyer, maybe they didn't like sex, or girls, or didn't know if they did, they were afraid and awkward, furtive about what they wanted. Those eyes would leave hers, lose hers, glance away, not look into her, not dare her, the way his did. He stared, glared, dared, he kept staring. It wasn't really arrogance. He was knowing. He knew something. She didn't know what he knew. She was eager and unsure.

Later, she could always tell who knew how to kiss, how to use his mouth, how to bite, how to hold her, by looking into his eyes and keeping the look and waiting for the glance into or away, she always knew. Her body was unruly. She was tremulous. She wanted to be lighter, fearless, and heavier, lustful, and freer, unburdened of an indeterminate weight she walked the world carrying. Her sexed body, unattended, sought attention. Attraction was received and sent ambivalently. She ached and tensed and didn't know why.

When he was sixteen, he didn't know what to do with his hands, where to put them, how hard to dig into her skin, did she like that, and he was mostly thinking about himself, his first time, and when he came, it was over and they'd done it, he'd gotten into her, her vagina was warm, kind of wet and velvety, and she didn't bleed that much. He didn't know if he loved her. But his friends said he didn't have to. He couldn't look at his mother, he knew she knew, and he wanted her to know, but he didn't want to tell her. He didn't see the girl again because she moved away. Maybe he wouldn't have anyway.

Later, he remembered the smell of her hair and the way she moved under his body and the way she didn't move. She made a sound, a little whimper. He didn't know what that was, pain, pleasure. He never stopped worrying about how heavy he was when he was on top of a woman. He never knew exactly what he expected from sex, women, from her, now. He wanted to feel good for longer than he did. He demanded stealthily. He suffered the loneliness of his own body.

She wasn't flying. She knew where she was. His hands and arms motioned down. Their gestures fell on the ground. Ecstasy's available, he laughed. Then he wanted to touch her. He was grimacing and smiling. He pointed again. She looked down. She was adamant. Literal minded. Blood rushed in her brain and pushed crazily through her body. It made thinking and orgasms possible.

He watched her. Her back was a ribbon of flesh, a river of flesh. He wasn't sure. He wanted her.

Someone else was another world.

Later, she wanted him.

She liked to lust, loved the sensation, the thrill, only when she could have what she wanted. She took a few chances. Sometimes she threw it away, let it go, risked everything, which wasn't much, she didn't care. She wasn't her body, she was. She couldn't tell about him yet, how he felt, how she felt about him.

He couldn't tell. He wouldn't tell.

Later, he entered her.

He said: You feel good.

He said: Do you think you could love me?

He said: Was that good?

He said: Did you come?

He said: I won't hurt you.

He said: Are you safe?

He said: Is this the right time?

He said: I don't go down on everyone.

He said: I don't know what's wrong with me.

He said: Are you bleeding?

He said: I think I could love you.

He said: Are you okay?

He said: Why did you do that?

He said: How do you like it?

He said: Did I hurt you?

He said: I really like you.

He said: Not now, give me some time.

He said nothing. He said a little. He said her name. He said everything he could. He couldn't talk.

She surrounded him. She took him in to her, let him in. The outsider's inside her, she thought and stopped herself. She didn't want to remind herself to forget. She looked at her body, his body. They were angling for position. They were imperfect pictures of people having sex. She bit him on the cheek.

He made love to her. She made love to him. She dangled above him. He fucked her, she fucked him, he relieved her, she frustrated him, he teased her, she tempted him. She waited. He moved. She grasped. He grabbed. She touched. He held. She clasped. He released. She contracted. He kneaded.

He closed his eyes. He opened his mouth wider. Wider and wider. He wanted to take her into him, swallow her. He looked funny to her, unfamiliar in his pleasure. He wondered what he looked like to her. He blanked the thought out, erased it. Fuck. His body jerked.

She wanted to bite him harder, even make him bleed, just a little. This won't hurt him, she thought. She didn't. She licked his shoulder, tentatively.

She was strange to him, a stranger. He was new to her but she could get used to him.

She said: You don't have to say anything.
She said: I like that.
She said: Do that again.
She said: No, not yet.
She said: Yes.
She said: I have a condom.
She said: Wait.
She said: I like you, too.
She said: It's been a while.
She said: I wish I knew you.
She said: That's all right.
She said: Are you crying?
She said: Again.
She said: Almost.
She said: You tell that to all the girls.
She said: Do what?
She said: Do it again.
She said: That doesn't hurt.
She said: That hurts.
She said: That feels good.
She said: Kiss me.
She said: Now.

In the universe of things she didn't know, sex was at the top of a long, unwritten list. Momentary, temporary, ever present, absent, disruptive, expected, it fled scrutiny. She didn't know if she'd ever find out. What wasn't named, named it.

A whisper, a moan, a stifled groan, lips parted, mouths opened and shut, like doors and windows. With sound. Without sound.

Talk to me, he said, say anything. He bore down on her. She didn't know what it meant. She was open to him. She confused him. He was alive and easier, heady. He was full. He didn't want to be empty. Later, it might make sense.

In the universe of things he didn't know, sex was a series of questions with good and bad in the answers. How good was he supposed to be, how good was it supposed to be, how bad is bad, how often is good, how long is good, how hard is good, how gentle is bad. It was always simple and immediate when he wanted it, and when he got it, it wasn't, and he wasn't, adequate or inadequate.

She looked at his face. His eyes were closed. His eyes were narrowed. His lips were clenched. Now they were curled. His hands were open, palms up. He was raw. His teeth showed. He chewed her lips, his lips. His upper lip stuck to his teeth. He muttered wordlessly. He threw his head back and forth. He rocked.

He put his hand under her thigh and flipped her over as if she were a leaf. She felt weightless, inconsequential. She wanted to be just a body. She didn't know if she could be. She didn't know what just a body was unless it was the idea, just a body.

She tickled his back. She was lazy. He placed both hands

under her ass and turned her again. She let him and threw her
leg over his hip and made it impossible for him to move. She was
stronger than he thought she was. She held him tight. He liked
that. He thought he liked that.

He looked at her face. He didn't see her pleasure. He took his
in violent spasms. She snatched hers from the wings of defeat.
Her pleasure was a mighty trophy.

He was freezing. She was looking away. He didn't know what
she saw.

He said: Are you cold?
He said: Want something to drink?
He said: Next time we'll go to your place.
He said: I have to sleep.
He said: Want to go out?

He pulled up the blanket and covered himself. He didn't
know what she wanted next. She didn't, either. He didn't know
what he wanted next. She didn't know what came next. The
aftermath was awkward and familiar.

She said: What time is the clock set for?
She said: I have to piss.
She said: I need a drink.
She said: I couldn't sleep now.

Naked, alone, or with him, she wasn't unencumbered, didn't
feel natural or unnatural. It was weird, lying there, bare and not

stripped of anything important. She felt blinded, blinkered, by her nakedness, less capable, more vulnerable and less. If she had muscles all over her body, like a bodybuilder, muscles like small, implacable breasts, she'd be impregnable.

Naked, with her, he was modest. Then he was unconcerned about his nakedness. He studied her. He liked her body, then he didn't. He wanted her to admire him. He wanted her not to care about his body. He hoped she'd take it and him for granted, almost. Embarrassed, casual, he rolled around in bed clownishly. She was harder, he thought, tougher than he liked. She wasn't perfect. He changed position. She changed in front of his eyes.

She changed position. She avoided his body. Then she stared at him, it. His penis was coiled, recoiled, returned to him. He blended into the bed sometimes. She might not really like him. He was softer than she thought he'd be. He was different from the way he seemed outside.

What happened wasn't visible.

What wasn't apprehended stayed defiant, resistant. It was obscene, how they felt and thought, and the obscene ran with the ecstatic, raced away, right out the door, right out the window, right out the frame, on a road to nowhere.

She said: I have a lot of work.
She said: Maybe tomorrow.
She said: I'll call you.
She said: I don't know.

He said: Later.

He said: When will I see you again?

He said: I'm really behind.

He said: No rush.

Being on the street was strange. It was hard to talk. They walked away from each other. The absence of sex, a fast intimacy, could become the source of a dirty joke or despair. Everyone wants to be happy.

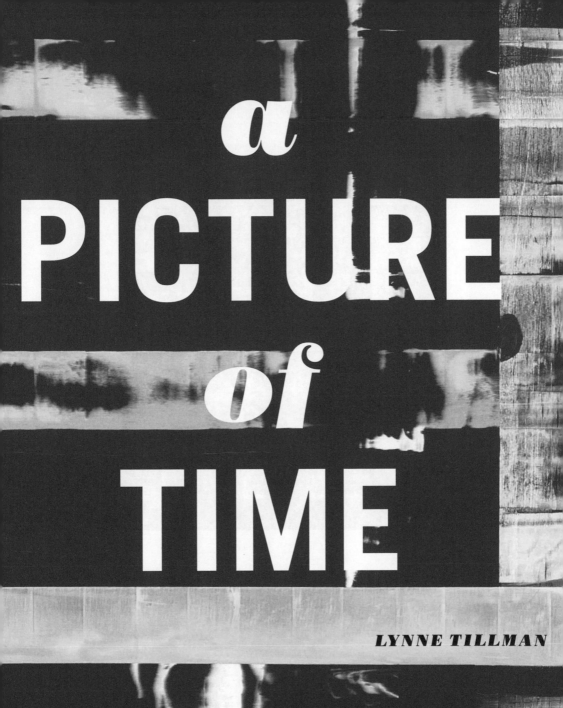

a
PICTURE
of
TIME

LYNNE TILLMAN

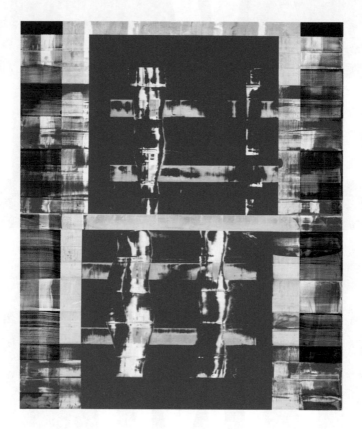

Stephen Ellis, Untitled, *1993. Oil and alkyd on linen.
72 x 60 inches. Private collection.*

A PICTURE OF TIME

You say there's no time like the present. But what is the present here? I've watched TV for ages and seen movies since I was three. TV's daily life and movies are a communal fantasy. Today is in color, yesterday's in black and white, and there's no agreement about tomorrow.

I hear music everywhere, and then there are voices. Everyone's speaking in a flow and rush of language, the words are like water. There are echoes, too. And I know the whispering won't stop. It's the past. Time passes on and fools us by living underneath the surface.

You say there's a reality we all exist in, and I say I won't agree to it. You become red, enraged, and I make something from that. Red becomes an opening, surprising you. But I put it in the corners, where its brilliance is held in suspension. I keep explosive red, like time, to myself. I keep it, like dreams and wishes, for myself.

I suppose it's obvious. I'm always fighting time. It's relentless in its mission, and I'm nothing to it. But there's no time in dreams, which is why I need them. There's protracted suspense, the ragged drama of discontent and tempestuous wishes. And morose blue may suddenly pop up, disguised as threat, to announce the predatory present. I may be able to appease it, the blues, if I can find a place to put it. Even in dreams I want to control sadness and danger. I surround and contain them, and later everything catches up with me.

You say take hold of yourself. I hold on to dear, difficult life and keep track of success and failure—and loss, the holes and emptinesses where I could fall off and forget the world. Oases and shelters beckon, tempting illusions wrapped in bars and stripes. I reach them and take the time to think about what to do next.

Time moves on without my consent. I should have known better. My schemes might be planted next to startling green thoughts and in earthy, black fields. If I'm lucky, the dark is rich and compassionate and will let me rest for a while. Something good might come along.

Is it judgment I'm awaiting or mercy? I don't know. I draw a broad line around myself and make a fortress against inevitability. Suddenly there's static, an impish, contentious energy I never expect. It disrupts connections, compelling me to assimilate forces I don't fully comprehend. Like electricity, which I've never stopped relying upon. I know it was discovered and had to be captured, even subdued. Yet it was always there, and it probably wasn't waiting, the way I am.

You're naked, you say. Protect yourself. I cover myself in shame, lust, and greed, smearing and hiding the humiliating marks of battle. I've done this many times and have become a funny kind of palimpsest. You say no one can escape, and I run down a narrow, single-minded trail. I burrow deep and throw on another layer, for warmth or as a palliative. I grow big and orange. Fire is more orange than red and, like anger, throws off more heat than light. When it dies, there are embers and ash, wan reminders of its glory. The sky becomes night and swallows everything. The night is a thrilling action figure in the human theater. I hide in the dark.

You say I can't fight the inevitable. But what else is there to fight? I arrive at my destination and tremble at reason's door. It's inviting to enter, seductive, but there's really not enough room. Still I've learned I can't be an exception and walk in through the back door. To outfox reason's complacency, I escort the unpredictable unconscious. As usual no one notices. Later, perpetually, everyone's surprised.

You and I watch the current match between rationality and irrationality. I bet on what we can't know, which wrestles with everyone's limits and confounds certainty. It usually claims victory, and tonight I win easily. There was more behind the scenes than we ever appreciated. You're sorry to lose, and I console you. But the truth is I applaud the victory and prefer it to reason's insensible claims. Like the one that says time heals all wounds. Time's no cure, no doctor. You and I go on. We continue somehow, and our persistence is the source of everything we make. I want to surrender, but I can't, and I live in that paradox, and so do you.

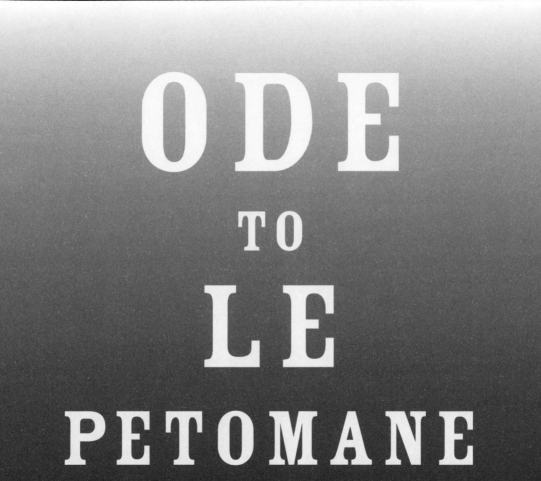

Roni Horn, Between Visibility and Nonexistence,
*1992. Gouache on paper. 18¹/₂ x 25³/₄ inches. Courtesy
of Matthew Marks Gallery.*

ODE TO LE PETOMANE

shuddered. I seemed. I wanted. I tried. I loved. I proposed. I discovered. I knew. I studied. I dug. I needed. I imitated. I believed. I was. I realized. I wanted. I had. I became. I initiated. I gushed. I declared. I recorded. I recognized.

I shuffled the deck. It was given to me, but I colored the cards. I dealt a hand. I threw the cards in the air. They fell on the floor. I picked them up in no special order. Failure hung around, pale, shapeless, ready.

I fox fate, it's a daily routine.

The wind's crazy. People walk, their umbrellas collapse. I can't fight the elements. I'm alone, watching. Another ugly brown shoe was lying at the back door this morning. It matches the one that dropped there last week in the middle of a wet, dark, wild night. I wasn't waiting for the other shoe to drop, then it did. My expectations are my own, sometimes I share them. Sometimes I'm disappointed or surprised. Expectations are secrets. I play with mine, them. It's a tricky business.

Fourteen ugly brown shoes could be sitting at the back door tomorrow. Maybe there was a party. Everyone took off their shoes. The shoes fell from the roof and landed at the back door. If fourteen bodies were lying there, dead, I'd need other explanations. A séance on the roof; they left their bodies behind. Or a mass suicide. I'd want to scream Murder, call the cops, if death was skulking at my door.

The shiny bags of garbage scattered in the backyard shimmer in the occasional sunlight. They sometimes look like a novel form of aboveground burial. The wind blows the bags everywhere. They've always been there. No one removes them, and I'm not going to touch them. I hate garbage, full of morbid ideas, crap.

Now a thin, tall guy is walking down the street, bent by the wind. He has to go to the post office and stand on line, negotiate with people who hate their jobs. The way he sees it, it makes him a kind of human retrospective—writing letters, walking to the post office, being willing to stand and wait patiently.

I engage with things as much as people. But I usually don't have fantasies about them. That probably isn't true. I watch television, I talk to it, it's not only talking to me. I'm not a sieve. It isn't, either. Something else could be there but that doesn't mean what's there isn't conclusive, in its way. Inconclusive too.

This tall, thin guy liked envelopes. Envelopes enveloped, and usually words were incommensurate. He folded the letter into three equal parts, the way nothing ever is, with definite edges, and stuffed it perfectly into the envelope. He sealed it up. He didn't hate licking glue. It reminded him he had a tongue like other animals who use it more. Letters usually reach their destination, and unseen by others, are read in private. Often the recipient doesn't really get the message. He knew that. It was a more controlled exchange even with the interference of the post office. If it's not the post office, it's the telephone company. He couldn't control that.

I don't come to any conclusions alone, even when I'm held in my own silly, irrelevant isolation. I think my isolation isn't solitary, it's a concoction—you're in it, so is he, she, they are too. You might have other ideas. You and I can appear to be interchangeable, easy to substitute. Like pronouns, just as deceptive. I can believe, pretend I'm volunteering. I renew myself, things. If I tremble, it's a disease. Nostalgia for the new.

The thin guy wrote his longtime fiancé, "We share heaven and hell. Hell's being right and wrong. You think I betray you by my indecision. It's how you think. What can I say. I'm vanishing imperceptibly."

A cranky magic act. The guy in the post office often disappeared behind the horizon between himself and others. He couldn't tell where the edge was for somebody else. For her. He pushed at her limits regularly. Cunning, silent, he demolished raw feelings which arrived from a purple nothing, a needy nonplace. They rushed out in clumps and wanted something to hang on to. Finders, keepers, weepers, his words were held responsible.

Now he was almost at the head of the line, worried about how he'd written her. He knew there was trouble ahead. He inevitably thought that, a record stuck in its own, ancient groove.

Your cover songs and mine could be danceable, fast, slow, permeable, intransigent, opaque, accessible, beautiful, reluctant, funny, tough, different from what's in store. I want to go far and still stay in touch, on line. I don't have a dog, but I could walk one mentally if I decided to. No one would know I was just walking the dog. I can more easily do the laundry dramatically. In the laundromat, MTV's on, I see other people's clothes, I watch their eyes, mouths, how they fold their shirts, they notice me or don't, smile, don't. Music caresses, pounds, a rhythm for everything. We're doing laundry in the same time, even if we're in different cycles. It's intimate and alien. Underpants flop around in dryers. That's anonymity. Signs hang on walls and doors. I always forget which dispenser is for the bleach. I approach the attendant, a woman with sweat on her lip, annoyance on her tongue, acid in her stomach. I smile, tame her fury temporarily, find out, pour in the bleach, go home, come back.

He thought hard about what to say, how to put it, what shapes and colors to use when he tried to draw it out for her, even how to sign the letter. His effort exposed him. When Dorothy Parker was restless, or lonely, she hung a one-word sign on her office door. MEN. Men walked in, thought it was the men's room. She laughed probably, enlivened. He had never thought of that—WOMEN. On his door. And he wouldn't, ever. He was surprised by what was immediate to him, but wasn't to other people. Same way around, them to him, her to him. His jaw ached sometimes, explaining, and he hated the sound of his own voice, repeating himself in different settings. All the words in his universe taunted him, pictures multiplied forever in a series of mirrors. Even his reasoning was an image of itself, feeding back. He was often, he was now, frightened for no reason. Outside the wind blew indifferently.

I change, don't, can't, have habits, am a habit, want to make everything flip into another register, can't find the register. Someone I knew once worked at the reception desk at Claridge's. A man called up and said, "There's a bomb in the hotel," and my friend opened the hotel register and looked for the name and answered, "I'm sorry, there's no Mr. Ahbomb in the hotel." Then he hung up. Later he realized it was a bomb threat.

You try to reach me, with reflections and illuminations, and I might not find what's evident to you. It's scary, this strangled distance between us, worrying about agreeing to agree even about the terms of agreement. Something may be avoided in the contract. It may be implicit, elusive, but necessary.

Sometimes I think that's all I can do—leave room. I build a room. I paint it, wallpaper it, furnish it, sleep in it, leave it, return to it, hope the room's still there. There's litter in it. I don't mean to return to garbage, but there's a lot of waste in my life.

The guy was staring at a man in the post office who had twenty packages to mail and was holding up the line. A robber stealing time. At least he was next. He wondered if his letter was to her or for her, or for someone else. Or for no one. He glanced back at the long snake of people with envelopes in their hands. Their vulnerability was on display. In that instant, he understood that a letter stands for something which has many letters in it. He wasn't sure if he was standing for himself and others, or not.

In the 19th century a French performer named Le Petomane farted for the public. He set his farts on fire, too, to give the audience a good show, an olfactory night on the town. I have a picture of Le Petomane, ass sticking out, long unlit wooden match in his hand. There must be a slit or opening in his trousers so he won't get burned. Hell of an entertainer. I wonder how he got the idea to go public.

The guy listened to his stomach growl. At home he let his body go, heard it compose a soundtrack—groans, sighs, moans, farts. He took painful, heavy breaths. He belched, chomped, chewed, slurped, smacked. No one compared slurps, belches, and groans, the beauty of life's secret, disgusting moments. His turn finally came. The postal worker he liked whispered, "Did you hear about the crash? Everyone was killed."

If weirdness was usual, expected, I'd be forced to think on my feet and sitting down. Make things up on the spot—dialogue, ways to walk, look, relationships. Nothing would correspond to anything for long. In a private arena, I'd have my own agenda. I wouldn't hurt anyone. See, I'm walking to the point, along the edge, where a fantasy of doing whatever I like and a drive to be liked compete. I'm not unique, so I don't have to worry. But in the present, I can't decide how many people I should speak to.

The guy shook his head, just grunted to the postal worker who had whispered about the devastating crash. Strangers share the grotesque. A shadow crossed over the envelope, it was the postal worker's hand. But the guy felt darkness, a gap, in the middle of his brain. She could've been killed on that flight. It was possible. Maybe he wanted her to die. He enjoyed the fantasy and tasted the sensation, bittersweet loss. Anguish and relief played a wistful song in him.

He mailed the letter. He wouldn't know how beautiful flesh was, he realized, until he couldn't touch hers anymore. He couldn't know how beautiful flesh was. He recorded all of this and more, and he wrote her again and again, "I can't. I won't." He invented a virtual reality game—a funeral home and cemetery for love. He stole and was stolen from, he deceived and was deceived. Don't try to contact me, she wrote back. Ever. She thought he was crazy.

I listen to Archbishop Desmond Tutu on the radio. He admits, sheepishly, "I love to be loved." I'm amazed by how many ways there are to go and how many dead ends. I can't try everything. I want to. I'm improvising, everything's provisional.

By now the thin guy was such a wreck, his gums were bleeding. He finished work at the insurance company. He locked the doors, turned on the burglar alarm, looked down the street, and glanced warily at some other men who stared vacantly at him. He turned his back. He saw the ocean, sullen and green. The grey sky was perpetually monotonous. Then the ocean roared. A huge flock of birds, thousands of black marks, dark ideas, streaked across the sky. He watched them swirl and dart. They flew in unison. They broke away from each other. They swelled and dropped and swooned. They rushed, scrambled, and took their shape again. Then they abandoned it and separated. They went on and on. He wondered why they did that. Things never total up. They never stay still.

Yesterday morning a man with a red nose and a face cut from too many close shaves removed the shiny garbage bags from the backyard. He had to climb through a window to get outside because the door wouldn't open. It wasn't locked, but it was stuck. When he couldn't get the door open, he cursed it. Then he turned and shot me a creepy, even sinister, half smile. He said, "I don't know what you're doing. But you've jinxed the place." I didn't say a word. If that's what he wants to think, let him. There are a million other explanations, but he must like the idea, be invested in it. It's not my bank, but I could begin to appreciate, investigate, his characterization, throw a party for it—a bad recognition is better than none at all, distorted mirrors still reflect an image. I have my illusions, he has his. I would stop celebrating loss, if I could figure out what replaces it.

The plumber has just left. He said he told the man with the red nose months ago that the door was stuck, the faucet needed to be fixed, the toilet seat was broken. I didn't jinx the place. It was already jinxed. I arrived, saw the damage, demanded repairs, got them. There are promises and mistakes everywhere. It's hard to tell them apart. I keep going.

LYNNE TILLMAN

Diller & Scofidio, Suitcases au Gogo, *1991.*
Mixed media. Collection of the artists.

LUST FOR LOSS

What gives value to travel is fear.... This is the most obvious benefit of travel.

—ALBERT CAMUS

Though she didn't really like to travel, Madame Realism often wanted to be someplace other than home. Travel caters to the uncanny, to impulse and serendipity, and Madame Realism took chances. She gambled away some of the time allotted to her in life, and defiantly, almost wantonly, acknowledged and nurtured a craving to wreck her own schedule and daily routine. I am my own homewrecker; it is one of my freedoms, she told herself.

To Madame Realism the self-inflicted habits of a typical day were no comfort. She disliked the idea of a typical day. Though habits afford a reliable sanity, Madame Realism resented her own customs. She even resisted them, as if they were the amorous advances of a former lover. Easy, but who needs it, she thought. I'd rather be sitting on a crowded train, next to smokers, living dangerously.

Tainted by wanderlust, resigned to a permanent tourism, Madame Realism plotted journeys she might take. She indulged a fantasy, like envisioning a movie she longed to see, then set it into motion, which was akin to that movie appearing on the screen. First there was a desired setting and then there was an outcome, a reality—a hotel, a museum, an avenue, a beach, a cafe—all of which she'd conjured before. After all, Madame Realism mused, when you're watching a movie, it's your reality.

But she suffered the pangs of most thrillseekers—she hated departures. After one particularly lugubrious leave taking, she observed that train stations and airports were, like graveyards, watering holes for the sentimental. Or the mournful. She suspected that people who hung around might be waiting for no one or nothing but a good cry. There were always reasons to cry, she knew, but not as many places to cry as reasons.

I like it when I don't know where I am, or why, but it also terrifies me, she admitted to herself. Madame Realism was taking off, running away, going on a vacation or just roaming. Her destination was the coast of Normandy. She was curious about World War II—she was definitely a postwar character—and had, if not a valid reason to be there, a valid passport. With it and money, she could get out of town. But just as she was suspicious of the reasons for following a routine, she was suspicious of the reasons for disrupting it.

Unsettled by her own vagueness, Madame Realism threw a bottle of aspirin into a bag. She tossed in another pair of underpants, too. The black silk underpants were an afterthought, a last-minute decision. Maybe all my decisions are, she worried, then closed her suitcase. She hummed an ancient tune: "Pack up your troubles in your old kit bag . . ." And do something. But she couldn't remember the lyrics. And what is a kit bag? She hesitated and cast last-minute glances about the room.

Madame Realism couldn't know what lurked around the corner, at home or abroad. From reading travel books and maps, from studying histories of particular locations, she could plan a course of action. But actually she yearned to be out of control in a place where she didn't know a soul. It's better to be a cliché, a reprehensible image, than not to venture forth, not to take a risk, she contended as she walked out of her apartment. Madame Realism might be both Sancho Panza and Don Quixote. She might also be their horse.

After having been asked by an airline representative if anyone had packed for her, if she was carrying a gift from a stranger, if she had left her suitcase unattended, Madame Realism boarded the plane, settled into a seat, and nervously considered, as the jet shot into the sky, what a first-minute decision might be. A decision of the first order. A crucial, life and death decision, which would certainly be made during war. That's why I'm going to Normandy, she concluded. To be alive in a place haunted by death and by great decisions. If that was true, if that was her motivation, Madame Realism felt even more peculiar and unreasonable.

What explains this mass mania / to leave Pennsylvania?

—Noel Coward

In a hotel not far from the beach, Madame Realism was standing on a small balcony. She was gazing out at the sea. Large, white cumulus clouds dotted the blue sky. The Channel changed from rough to smooth in a matter of hours. She found herself watching the rise and fall of the waves, the rush and reluctance of the tides, with fascination or dread. Or concern. Which characterization was most true she was not sure. Truth was so difficult to be told, small and big truths, she could never tell it completely. Much as she might try, she couldn't even adequately define the weird anguish she experienced at the sight of the placid stretch of beach that touched the sea. The five beaches of Operation Overlord—Juno, Omaha, Sword, Gold, Utah. She had memorized their wartime names. The code names intrigued her, codes always did.

The light blue water—maybe it was more green than blue— grew progressively darker as it left the shore. The sea was always mysterious, ever more so with depth. Unfathomable, she reminded herself, the way the past is as it becomes more distant and unreadable with every day, every day a day further away from the present or the past, depending upon the direction from which one is thinking. But is something that is regularly described as a mystery, like the ocean, like history, mysterious?

Puzzled, Madame Realism was never less contemporary than when she traveled. Each journey was the fulfillment of a desire, and desire is always an old story. Like everyone else's, Madame

Realism's desires were born and bred in an intransigent past. Even if she imagined herself untethered as she flew away, she was tied. When she journeyed to an historic site especially, she kept a date with history. And when she trafficked in history, she was an antique. At least she became her age or recognized herself in an age.

Spread on the bed were histories and tourist brochures of the region. Military strategy appealed to her; secretly she would have liked to have been privy to the goings on in one of the D-Day war rooms. But there hadn't been any women in them. I'd have to rent a war room of my own, she laughed, and then recollected, in a rapid series of images, the war movies she'd consumed all her life—*Waterloo Bridge, The Best Years of Our Lives, The Longest Day, The Dirty Dozen.* Celluloid women waited and worried about men. They were nurses, wives, secretaries. Sometimes they drove ambulances, sometimes they spied. They grieved, they loved. Madame Realism learned from a TV program that the first woman to land on the Normandy beachhead at Omaha was an American named Mabel Stover, of the Women's Army Corps. Mabel Stover, earnest and robust, appeared on the program, exhorting World War II veterans to contribute money to a U. S. memorial, a "Wall of Liberty." "Your name belongs on this wall," she exclaimed. "It's your wall. Go for it, guys and gals."

> *You receive unforgettable impressions of a world in which there is not a square centimeter of soil that has not been torn up by grenades and advertisements.*
>
> —KARL KRAUS

Early the next morning, restless and sleepless, Madame Realism left the hotel and went for a walk on the beach. There was hardly any-one around. The sea was choppy. With each barefoot step on the sand—the tide was out—Madame Realism concocted a battle story: Here a man had fallen. He broke his leg, he struggled, and a soldier he never saw before helped him, then he was shot. Both were shot, but both lived, somehow. Or, here someone died. But without pain, a bullet to the brain. Or, here a soldier was brave and sacrificed himself for another, but lived. They both lived. Or, here a man found cover and threw a grenade that knocked out an enemy position. Or, here someone was terrified, sick with fear, and could not go on.

At the phrase "sick with fear," Madame Realism kicked her foot in the sand and uncovered a cigarette butt. She wondered how long it had been buried. It was trivial to contemplate in a place like this, even absurd. But I can't always control what I think, she thought.

Madame Realism jarred herself with vivid images of thousands of soldiers rushing forward on the beach. She thought about the men who had been horribly seasick in the boats that carried them to shore. On D-Day, years ago, the weather was bad and the sea was rough. Madame Realism looked again at the water and toward the horizon. Imagine being sick to your guts and being part of the greatest armada in history, imagine being aware that you were making history in the moment it was happening, imagine having the kind of anonymous enemy who is deter-mined to kill you—or being a terrifying enemy yourself. In the next moment she scolded herself: If you're throwing up over the side of a boat or scared to death, you're not thinking about history. You're just trying to stay alive.

At the horizon the sea was severed from the sky, or it met the sky and drew a line. As she did when she was a child, Madame Realism speculated about what she could not see, could never see, beyond that line, that severe border. She squinted her eyes and stood on her toes, hoping to see farther. It was impossible to know how far she actually saw. Still, she lingered and meditated upon the uncanny meeting of water and air, how it was and wasn't a meeting, how the touch of the air on the sea wasn't like the touch of a hand to a brow, or a mouth to a breast. It wasn't a touch at all. Just another pathetic fallacy. The sky doesn't kiss the sea. Jimi Hendrix must have been wildly in love or high when he wrote that line, "'scuse me while I kiss the sky."

Madame Realism licked her lips and tasted the salt on them. She loved that. She always felt very much alive near the ocean. She breathed in deeply. It was strange to be alive, always, but stranger to feel invigorated and happy in a place where there had been a battle, a life and death struggle. Maybe it wasn't weird, she consoled herself. Maybe it's like wanting to have wild sex right after someone dies.

Life wants to live, a friend once told her. Especially, Madame Realism thought, digging her toes into the sand, in a place where it was sacrificed. Death wasn't defeated here, but victory transformed it. That was the hope, anyway. Hope disconcerted Madame Realism. It was just the other side, the sweet side, of despair.

The soldiers landing, the planes dropping bombs, the guns shooting, the chaos, the soldiers scrambling for safety—she could envision it. But an awful gap split her comprehension in half, much like the sea was divided from the sky. It split then from now, actuality from memory, witnesses from visitors.

From time to time, Madame Realism forgot herself, but she was also conscious of being in the present. She was aware that time was passing as she reflected on time past. But even if she had not lived through it, the war lived through her. She was one of its beneficiaries; it was incontrovertible, and this was her war as much or even more than Vietnam.

Of course, she told herself, it's odd to be here. The past doesn't exist as a file in a computer, easy to call up, manage and engage. We can't lose it, though we are, in a sense, lost to it or lost in it. But was WWII being lost every day? she wondered. Everything was changing and had changed. The former Yugoslavia, the former Soviet Union, a reunified Germany. She recalled Kohl and Reagan's bitter visit to Bitburg. Was the end of the Cold War a return to the beginning of the century and an undoing of both world wars? It wasn't cold now, but Madame Realism trembled. Once history holds your hand, it never lets go. But it has an anxious grip and takes you places you couldn't expect.

And the wall of old corpses. / I love them. / I love them like history.
                                                                —Sylvia Plath

Suddenly Madame Realism realized that there were many people around her, speaking many different languages. Tourists, just like her. She shrugged and marched on. I go looking for loss and I always find it, she muttered to herself, a little lonely in the

crowd. She reached Omaha beach and the enormous U.S. cemetery. The rows and rows of gravestones were rebukes to the
living. That's precisely what entered her mind—rebukes to the
living. She shook her head to dislodge the idea. Now, instead
of rebuke, a substitute image, sense or sensation—all the graves
were reassurances, and the cemetery was a gigantic savings
bank with thousands of tombstonelike savings cards. Everyone
who died had paid in to the system and those who visited
were assured they'd received their money's worth. That's
really crazy, she chastised herself. Over seven thousand U.S.
soldiers were buried in this cemetery, and Madame Realism
knew not a soul. But what if the tombstones were debts, claims
against the living?

"I'd rather be," W.C. Fields had carved on his tombstone,
"living in Philadelphia." Sacreligious to the end, Field was outrageous in death. And surrounded by thousands of white tombstones,
Madame Realism was overwhelmed by the outrageousness of
death itself. But since she was only a visitor to it, death was eerily,
gravely, reassuring. Madame Realism looked at the dumb blue sky
and away from the aching slabs of marble. But when she reluctantly faced them again, they had become, for her, monuments
that wanted to talk. They wanted to speak to her of small events
of devotion, fearlessness, selflessness, sacrifice.

Markers of absence, of consequence, of heartbreak, of loss,
each was whispering, each had a story to tell and a silenced
narrator. Madame Realism was astonished to be in a ghost story,
spirited by dead men. But it was a common tale. Everyone
hopes the dead will speak. It's not an unusual fantasy, and

perfect for this site, even site specific, in a way. Though maybe, Madame Realism contemplated, they choose to be silent. Maybe in life they didn't have much to say or didn't like talking. Maybe they had already been silenced. What if they don't want to start talking now? That was a more fearsome, terrible fantasy. In an instant, the tombstones stopped whispering.

More people joined her, to constitute, she guessed, a counter-phobic movement, a civilian army fighting against everyday fears. During the second world war, President Roosevelt had advised her nation: "There is nothing to fear but fear itself." War is hell, she intoned mutely, silent as a grave.

Haunted and ghosted, Madame Realism stared at the tomb-stones. The sun was shining on them, and they glared back at her. They glowered unhappily. And she had a curious desire. She wanted to sing a song, though she didn't have much of a voice. She wanted to sing a song and raise the dead. She wanted to dance with them. She wanted to undo death and damage. Even if it was a cliché, or she was, she gave herself to it. All desires are, after all, common, she reflected, and closed her eyes in ecstasy.

At last Madame Realism was spinning out of control in a place where she didn't know a soul. Maybe she was discovering what it meant to be transgressive. She wasn't sure, because that happened only when you couldn't know it. For a moment or two she dizzily abandoned herself to a god that was not a god, to a logic that was not logical. She imagined she'd lost something, if not someone. She had not lost herself, not so that she couldn't find herself again once she returned home. But she felt foolish or turned around, turned inside out or upside down. I'm just a fool to the past, she hummed off key, as the past warbled its siren song. And in a duet, and unrehearsed, Madame Realism answered its lusty call.

Lynne Tillman

This Is Not It

Juan Muñoz, Raining Room. *1994. Wood, glass, and water. Courtesy of the Estate of Juan Muñoz.*

THIS IS NOT IT

If I were only somewhere else than in this lousy world!
—Ludwig Wittgenstein

Whenever I arrive, it's the wrong time. No one has to tell me. The right time is a few minutes earlier or later. Invariably I arrive at the wrong time in the wrong place. Wherever I am, it is the wrong place. It's not where I should be. No one says a word when I arrive. I am always unexpected.

Because it's the wrong place, I want to be someplace else. I always want to be in the place where I should have been. The place where I should have been is paradise on earth. It is inaccessible to me, because I cannot arrive on time at the right place.

(I try to be still.)

Because wherever I am is not where I should be, I am always ill at ease. I'm in an uncomfortable position. I have conversations with the wrong people. I should not be speaking to them. They know this, but everyone is polite since each of them may be similarly indisposed. They never remark that my presence is a problem to them. They put up with me; I put up with them. I always wonder when I can leave gracefully. I'm never graceful, because I don't fit in wherever I am.

(I try to control myself.)

In the wrong place at the wrong time, the wrong people and I are obviously in a drama, a tragedy or comedy. Whatever tragedy I am in, unwittingly and involuntarily, it's not the right one for me. It's either too grand or pathetic, an exaggeration, considering my position or station, which is an impossible one. A neighboring tragedy, the one next door, would be better for me. But it is unavailable to me. It is doubtless the tragedy I was born to. But my tragedy would not be invigorated by comparison. Just the opposite. The emptiness at its center, with me as the wrong hero, makes it funny. People laugh at my dilemma. In someone else's tragedy, my dilemma would be acknowledged appropriately.

(I try to be unobtrusive.)

Whatever comedy I am in, whenever I inadvertently partic- ipate, it is being played by overly tragic people. It's the wrong comedy. I am unsuitably sad. I forget the punchlines and tell jokes badly, with the wrong timing. People cry at my ill-timed jokes. I cry when I should laugh. When I am mistakenly in the audience, at someone else's tragedy or comedy, my reactions are consistently wrong.

(I try to leave.)

Whenever I attempt to go, I ask a friend which is the right way. But whoever is my friend is the wrong friend. This is not the person who should be my friend. Even if this person is a friend, he or she may provide the wrong advice. Or this friend may tell me to find the information I need in a book.

(I try to be sensible.)

Whatever book I find is the wrong book. The right book is on the shelf, in the bookstore or library, next to the wrong one I discover. Once I have it and begin to read it, I know it's the wrong book. No wrong book will tell me what I need to know, but I keep buying and reading books. I buy the same books again and again. Because I put them away in the wrong place, I forget I already have them.

(I try to find myself.)

Whenever I flee to a place I think I've never been, I discover that I've been there before. I hated the place on my first visit, but I've repressed the memory of it. I return to hated places often. I have seen many movies again, too. I go twice to places and to see people and movies I should never have visited or seen in the first place.

(I try to abstain.)

Whenever I see myself in a mirror, I don't believe the person is me. I believe I'm seeing the wrong person. This person masquerades as me. This person apes me. I try to catch this person unaware by sneaking up to surprise the mirror image. I am always disappointed when the wrong person shows up. The wrong person consistently makes the wrong appearance.

(I try not to trust appearances.)

Since I am in the wrong place, it must be the wrong mirror. The wrong mirror must not mirror the right image. It can't be me. But I am disappointed never to see myself. I keep looking. I may simply be the wrong person.

(I try not to want to escape. I try not to cry or laugh. I try to remember. I try to act differently.)

If I am the wrong person, this must be why, whatever world I am in, there is a better one elsewhere. Whatever money I have, more money is waiting somewhere else. This is why I do not like what I see. It is why I don't want what I have and why I want what is nearby.

Whatever I have is not what I should have. Whatever makes me happy ultimately makes me sad. I am the wrong person living my life. Someone somewhere else must be better off.

(I try to fool myself.)

Whoever I am, I am wrong. I try not to expect anything. It's impossible not to expect the wrong things in life. But I can't expect nothing. Nothing's certain. This may be wrong.

(I try not to jump to conclusions.)

Flowers

LYNNE TILLMAN

Vik Muniz, FREESIA REFRACTA (FREESIA), 1998. From
FLOWERS. *Gelatin silver print. 11 x 13¹/4 inches.*
Courtesy of the artist.

FLOWERS

Flowers are not teeth.
Flowers are not beef.
Flowers are not beets.
Flowers are not grief.
Flowers are not neat.
Flowers are not birds.
Flowers are not beds.

Flowers don't think.

Flowers are not beasts.
Flowers are not breasts.
Flowers are not books.
Flowers are not brooks.
Flowers are not cream.

Flowers are not crime.
Flowers are not screams.
Flowers are not rings.

Flowers don't drool.

Flowers are not singers.
Flowers are not music.
Flowers are not fiends.
Flowers are not fences.
Flowers are not braces.
Flowers are not races.
Flowers are not heaven.

Flowers don't phone.

Flowers are not bread.
Flowers are not foolish.
Flowers are not hopeful.
Flowers are not pain.
Flowers are not rain.
Flowers are not parks.
Flowers are not cars.
Flowers are not stupid.

Flowers don't talk.

Flowers are not bunnies.
Flowers are not Broadway.
Flowers are not cunning.
Flowers are not tough.
Flowers are not soap.
Flowers are not movies.
Flowers are not wits.

Flowers don't moan.

Flowers are not rhymes.
Flowers are not time.
Flowers are not crazy.
Flowers are not tragedy.
Flowers are not bugs.
Flowers are not sinks.
Flowers are not drinks.
Flowers are not enough.

Flowers don't listen.

Flowers are not satan.
Flowers are not waiting.
Flowers are not water.
Flowers are not tubs.
Flowers are not grubs.

Flowers are not doors.
Flowers are not easy.

Flowers don't dance.

Flowers are not windows.
Flowers are not widows.
Flowers are not pathetic.
Flowers are not prophetic.
Flowers are not tenants.
Flowers are not hopeless.
Flowers are not lovers.
Flowers are not understanding.

Flowers don't complain.

Flowers are not cars.
Flowers are not wrecks.
Flowers are not sex.
Flowers are not bears.
Flowers are not chairs.
Flowers are not guns.

Flowers don't care.

Flowers are not words.
Flowers are not one-liners.
Flowers are not one-night stands.
Flowers are not wrong.
Flowers are not right.
Flowers are not nothing.

MADAME REALISM
LIES HERE

Jeff Koons, Michael Jackson and Bubbles, *1988. Porcelain. 43 x 73 x 35 inches. Courtesy of The Dakis Joannou Collection, Athens.*

MADAME REALISM LIES HERE

Madame Realism awoke with a bad taste in her mouth. All night long she'd thrashed in bed like a trapped animal. The white cotton sheets twisted around her frenetic, sleeping body, and, like hands, nearly strangled her. Madame Realism pounded her pillow, beating it into weird shapes, and when finally she lay her head on it, she smothered her face under the blanket, to muffle the world around her. She wanted to tear herself from the world, but it was tearing at her. She wasn't ever sure if she was sleeping even when she was. Her unconscious escapades exhausted her. All restless night, her dreams plagued her, both too real and too fantastic.

She was in a large auditorium and a work of art spoke for her. Much as she tried, she couldn't control any of its utterances. Everywhere she went, people thought that what it said was the final word about her. When they didn't think it spoke for her, they thought it spoke about them. They objected violently to what it was saying and started fighting with each other—kickboxing, wrestling. The event was televised, and everything was available worldwide. It was also taped, a permanent record of what should have been fleeting. Mortified, Madame Realism fled, escaping with her life.

In another dream, a sculpture she'd made resembled her. It didn't look exactly like her, but it was close enough. Friends and critics didn't notice any significant differences. But she thought it was uglier. Still, what was beauty? ugliness? Maybe she'd done something to herself—a nose job or face lift, her friends speculated. But the statue was much taller—bigger than life, everyone said—with an exaggerated, cartoonish quality. People confused her with it, as if they were identical. Madame Realism kept insisting, We're not the same. But no one listened.

In the last, she took off her clothes repeatedly, and, standing naked in a capacious and stark-white, hospital-like room, where experiments and operations might be performed, she lectured on the history of art. To be heard, she told herself, she needed to be naked, to expose herself. Nakedness was honesty, she thought; besides she had nothing to hide. But no one saw that. They just saw her body. And it wasn't even her own. It was kind of generic.

Madame Realism rubbed the sleep out of her eyes. Everything was a test, each morning an examination. She was full of delinquent questions and renegade answers. In her waking life, as in her dreams, she concocted art that confronted ideas about art. So life wasn't easy; few people wanted to be challenged. But Madame Realism had principles and beliefs, though she occasionally tried to disown them, and her vanity made her vulnerable. What if she didn't look good? Still, she didn't want to serve convention, like a craven waiter, or fear being cheap and brazen, either.

Things had no regard for the claims of authors and patrons, and Madame Realism's work wasn't her child. But, inevitably, it was related to her, often unflatteringly. Sometimes she was vilified, as if she were the mother of a bad kid who couldn't tell the truth. But what if art can't tell the truth? What if it lies? Madame Realism did sometimes, shamelessly, recklessly. She remembered some of her lies, and the ones she didn't could return, misshapen, to undo her. Uncomfortable now, she stretched, and the small bones in her neck cracked. The body realigns itself, she'd heard, which comforted her for reasons she didn't entirely understand.

Sometimes, in overwrought moments, in her own mental pictures, where she entertained illusions, she made art—no, life—perform death-defying feats. It wiped out the painful past. Life quit its impetuous movement into unrecognizable territory. She herself brutally punched treacherous impermanence in the nose. In her TV movies, art took an heroic stand, like misguided Custer, defeated criminal mortality, and kept her alive, eternally.

But Madame Realism, like everyone else, knew Custer's fate. So it wasn't surprising that her late-night dates with Morpheus had turned increasingly frantic. She didn't believe in an afterlife, and those who did had never been dead.

What if, Madame Realism mused, finally arising from her messy bed with an acrid, metallic taste in her mouth, what if art was like Frankenstein? Mary Shelley's inspiration for Frankenstein was the golem, which, legend goes, was a creature fashioned from clay by a Rabbi Low in the 17th century. The figure was meant to protect the Jewish people. But once alive, the golem ran amok, turned against its creator, and became destructive. Rabbi Low was forced to destroy the golem.

Madame Realism walked creakily into the kitchen and filled the kettle with water. She put the kettle on the stove. She always did the same thing every morning, but this morning she felt awkward. Then she walked into the bathroom and looked at herself in the mirror. She discovered a terrible sight. What she had dreamed had happened. There was a cartoonish quality to her. All her features were exaggerated. Her breasts had disappeared and her chest tripled in size, her ass was so big she could barely sit on a chair. Her biceps were enormous, and she flexed them. It was strangely thrilling and terrifying.

Madame Realism started to scream, but what came out of her mouth was the first line of a bad joke: "Have you heard the one about the farmer's daughter?" She recited this mechanically, when she really meant to cry: This can't be happening. She tried to collect herself. She could be the temporary product of her own alien imagination. She could be a joke that wasn't meant to be funny.

Tremulous and determined, she walked into her studio—actually shuffled, for with so much new weight on her, she couldn't move as quickly as she once had. Carrying the burden of new thoughts, she reassured herself, was weird and ungainly. Just as soon as she said that to herself, all the art in her studio metamorphosed. It was not hers, but she recognized the impulse to make it. Still, she was shocked. She'd never used rubber or stainless steel before.

Then, like golems, these monstrous pieces—which is what she thought of the invaders—became animated. A large, inflatable flower pushed her into a chair. And her ass was so big, she fell on the floor. When she looked up, there was a ceramic double figure staring down at her. It was Michael Jackson and one of his pet monkeys. Michael was crying. She'd never seen him cry before. Then he said:

> Call me tasteless, it doesn't matter. What you expect to see is just as tasteless. What is taste? Educated love? Don't you love me? After all this time, don't you know me . . . aren't we friends? . . . Don't be surprised—I might be Michaelangelo's *David*. I am popular and so was *David*. He protected his people and fought Goliath and won.

Well, Madame Realism heard herself say aloud, do you know the one about. . . . She wanted to say something about ideas, but she couldn't stop kidding around.

Michael Jackson and his beloved monkey became silent, and suddenly she was overcome by a copulating couple. Madame Realism felt embarrassment creep over her new, big body. The lovers disengaged, and the beautiful woman spoke:

> Against death, I summon lust and love. Lust is always against death. It is life. Without my freely given consent

and with it, totally, I'm driven to mark things out of an existence that will end against its will. It's a death I cannot forge, predict, violate or annihilate. Ineluctable death is always at the center, and like birth the only permanent part of life, central to meaning and meaninglessness. And to this meaning and meaninglessness, I ask, Why shouldn't you look at us in the act of love? What happens to you when you do?

The sculpted male partner nodded in agreement. The couple moved off and threw each other to the ground.

Madame Realism knew the word pornography meant the description of the life and activities of prostitutes, of what was obscene, and that there were drawings of prostitutes' activities in orgy rooms back in ancient times. Even now, the rooms weren't supposed to be seen. But what shouldn't be seen, and why? Legendary New Yorker Brendan Gill, known as a man of taste, was asked why he watched pornography. He said: Because it gives me pleasure. Pleasure, Madame Realism said aloud, pleasure. Her biceps flexed.

With that, an enormous and brilliant painting appeared on the wall. Unlike the sculptures that had conversed with her, the painting remained mute. But it looked at her, it looked at her with an enormous unblinking eye, and it stared at her as if she were an object. It seemed to be the viewer, so she was being viewed by art. This had never happened before, she thought, with peculiar wonder. She felt naked in a fresh and violent way.

Art was a golem. It had taken over. It had a life of its own, and now she feared it was assessing her. What did it say about her? To be winning, she told it a joke, which more or less popped out of her mouth. But the painted eye kept looking. She followed its gaze and realized the painting wasn't really seeing her. She wanted it to, but it didn't. It stared past her, perhaps into the future or the past. It didn't speak, though maybe it spoke to her. It didn't offer an opinion of her. It said nothing at all about her. Nothing.

Madame Realism swooned and fainted. When she awoke, everything was as it had been in her studio. Her work was back in its place. She was no longer cartoonish.

She thought: My work can't protect me. I will be true to my fantasies, even when I don't recognize them. What I make is not entirely in my power, as conscious as I try to be. It's always in my hands and out of my hands, too. I like to look at things, because they make me feel good, even when they make me feel bad. I'm proud to be melancholic. I like to make things, because they usually make me feel good. I am not satisfied with the world, so I add to it. My desires are on display. What I make I love and hate.

Forever after, and this is strange to report, maybe unbelievable, Madame Realism saw things differently. Like Kafka's "Hunger Artist," who fasted for the carnival public who watched him waste away, until one day, when no one was looking or cared that he was starving, he wasted into nothing and died, she did what she wanted. She made a spectacle of herself from time to time, mostly in her work, trying to tell the truth and finding there's no truth like an untruth. She kept pushing herself to greater and greater joys and deprivations, which were invariably linked. And like any interesting artist, who can't help herself and is in thrall to her own discoveries, Madame Realism shocked herself most, over and over again.

James Welling, #51, 1999. Gelatin silver print.
52¹/8 x 38¹/8 inches. Edition of three. Courtesy of Donald
Young Gallery, Chicago. Collection of the artist.

SNOW-JOB

They took the slide down the well-used slope. He was slick, she was fast. They had a violent historical thirst and used one straw. It'd been an ice age.

They knew wanderlust and practiced wet looks. The chilly, movie-less nights made for simpler submission. They slipped into a crevice of their own making.

Why do you think I want you? he asked.

She feigned a tricky spin and a wink. He breathed on her eyes.

I like to climb mountains, he said irrelevantly.
I like to read faces, she said similarly.

Small talk, preparatory.

    Face reading? he asked languorously.
    An art or practice, maybe a craft, she said delicately.
    Oh yeah? he said.
    But it's hard to do in cold climates, she said. The cold keeps people's faces tight, restrained.

    Facial, glacial, he said.

And they both collapsed into fantasy.

He cut a few corners, racing, high, speaking wildness, and then he performed some fancy tongue turns. A flash display. She threw in several lurid words, moaned, stopping him short, almost blinding him. Thrusting against intrepid, ice-like reticence, they produced heat, and friction, too, of course.

Now they were melting at the speed of white light. A blizzard of steep cries, quick moves, slow words, and racy sighs resulted in the inevitable lacy, diaphonous wetness. His sweet, breathy language tongued inside her. She was gliding toward home base. Snowball coming. Yes. OK.

But then they noticed the drifts, aimless, dull, chaotic, until the fast drop, which was never really unexpected, just sudden, and— oh, the chasm's here. They had to separate, start over and turn back to the beginning.

White powder covered them theatrically. They were cold as statues, and their tracks had been erased. Next time they'd slide another way.

wild LIFE

LYNNE TILLMAN

Barbara Ess, NO TITLE, 1995. Color photograph.
40 x 60 inches. Courtesy of Curt Marcus Gallery.

WILD LIFE

The room was alive. I knew it better than my body. The whole house sighed and shuddered, breathing inaudibly through its doors and windows.

In and out, in and out I went, and one existence melted like snow into another. The sun was fierce and crazy. I cooled in green pools or under the shade of gracious trees. Beneath the stalwart moon, luminously impassive, I imagined the world. In my dreams, someone like me, a sprite, shimmered and danced, as dramatic as a noonday shadow. Day leaked into night, and going to bed was my first compromise.

Life spread itself before me, lay there like the backyard on a summer morning, the blacktop highway drifting out of town. I saw with my hands, envisioned with my skin, tasted with my eyes. At night the neighbors' houses shut their doors and lights, and I drew faces and pasted flowers and shells onto sheets of paper. I marked passing moments and kept mementoes, making sense of an immense unruliness. Even then I was captive, and it was uncapturable. So was I.

Laughter and fireworks, danger and whispering, skinned knees and fights delighted or stunned me, then metamorphosed into streaks of light and color, unstable images, and memory. All things had lives of their own, distinct from mine and part of mine, too. I was unformed, in a hurry, and always late. Time was the yellow school bus, waiting for me at the corner.

Intimations of death and freedom flirted and blinked knowingly. I lay on my back, conjuring tomorrow. The sky appeared to be my plate glass window to heaven. I'd go there if I were good. The grass smelled fresh and warm, and I didn't want to leave the earth. I dug my toes in the dirt, startling ants that marched industriously across my naked stomach. Occasionally I glimpsed the future, which was a secret. I'd have a dog, a figure, a job, know bad boys, read bad books, stay up late. People said I was a girl with promise. Cross your heart and hope to die.

When anonymous breezes caressed me, I trembled, and when finally the wind stirred me, I didn't know its name was lust. Longing was spectral. At first I was a spectator, but I was destined to become one of desire's permanent guests. What was wanting? Every inexperienced day, I sought experience and swore allegiance to myself. I practiced no science, though patterns were everywhere. I thought I concocted my own.

Time didn't wait forever, and I took the train out of town. I didn't intend to go back. Unpracticed, I learned lyrics to old songs: Walls don't keep secrets. Roads end. Hope's necessary. Bridges collapse. Love starts and stops. Promises are made to be broken. Shaken, I settled, only to discover the dictatorship of the temporary. Longing and time were constant, though, and they were companions in ravishment. But the past never diminished and was not impoverished. Still, I tried to save it, enrich it, and, more beggar and thief than savior, returned to it again and again.

LYNNE TILLMAN

dead sleep

Dolores Marat, Untitled, *n.d. Courtesy of the artist.*

DEAD SLEEP

He told himself not to be afraid of death. He told himself it would be like sleep, eternal and mindless, a pallid time without time and dreams. He told himself he hadn't known he wasn't alive when he wasn't, so death would simply come and carry him from sleep to sleep, and he'd never know life's absence or lost presence. It would be, he told himself, as if he'd never been born.

But ever since he was a child and comforted himself with these morbid thoughts, the relationship between nightly unconsciousness and the absolute end of consciousness undid him. He feared falling asleep because he might, he explained to his mother, wake up dead. He feared being cold and begged his father to promise to bury him in a coffin with a blanket and pillow. A bemused, somewhat anxious father acceded to his son's wishes. But his father was now dead and his mother ill; he was alone. There was no one he could trust to honor a childish request, to sit by his bed, hold his hand, or watch him as he drifted off.

No one could ever know where siren sleep would lead. Each night the man fought physiology's demands, pummeled his pillow, rose from his tormented bed, propped himself, like a puppet, at the window, wrote in his journal, an insomniac's bible, then returned, defeated, to his place of distress. On rare occasions sleep overwhelmed him, and he succumbed to its caresses as he might a lover he couldn't satisfy. During the day sleeplessness disoriented him. He forced himself to work, and his success as a criminal lawyer startled especially him. But his lovers abandoned him. After sex he was restless, and though each woman cajoled and reassured him, his absorbing obsession took over and consumed him. They were never part of it.

Finally he resorted to sleeping pills whose chemical ministrations he hadn't wanted before—another erratic element in tempestuous life. But without sleep he couldn't control his days, either. He had felt compelled to supplicate the demon god of night. The pills wore down his resistance; chemicals lit up his brain in strangely glowing neon patterns. During the first narcotized sleep, blood streamed in front of his eyes, and, upon waking, he imagined he'd gone to the theater and watched a horror movie. Still, a horrible vision was preferable to none.

Time passed irrevocably. The insolent pills by the side of his bed glowed at him. They had him now. Sleep could be his only through their agency. He had none. With an urgency and devotion new to him, he submitted and swallowed and gave himself over to the brightly colored capsules.

Slowly he started to love sleep, love it too much, like a slave who actually adored his master. He had let sleep defeat him, he told himself, it had needed help. But, in its silky arms, he didn't care.

Soon he didn't want to wake up. His long-playing dreams escorted him to places he would never have gone awake. He cavorted, unsexed and oversexed, with women and men, delighted in gore, and turned sullen and violent like an unexpected storm. He was an assassin, he was put to death and yet remained alive. He played the executioner who occasionally refused to push the button or wield the axe. Sometimes he quietly watched the dead, who now only looked asleep.

Sweet, thick sleep devoured him. He wanted it all the time, he could never get enough. Sleep before time, sleep before mother and father, sleep before love, sleep before discontent. Sleep a nation, a homeland, where his voice was his, not his, and everybody's. Sleep, heavy and brilliant and immense in its singular, lonely, fantastic universe, was preferable to every sensation the other existence extended to him.

The man stopped fearing death. He was free. He swallowed more and more pills. He lost all sense of conscious life, its happy and sad surprises, and when he woke up dead, he did not, of course, know it.

Madame Realism

LOOKS FOR RELIEF

LYNNE TILLMAN

Haim Steinbach, Untitled (Art Deco bust, display mounts, necklaces), *1989. Plastic laminated wood shelf, plaster bust, glass and plastic costume jewelry, and velvet upholstered cardboard display stands. 12¹/₂ x 103 x 10¹/₂ inches. Collection of Sudwestdeutsche Landesbank, Stuttgart. Courtesy of David Lubarsky.*

MADAME REALISM
LOOKS FOR RELIEF

The sultry nights stretched credulity. Madame Realism stood up from the table and pushed her chair into a corner. She had been sitting in one position for too long and had become stiff. Her body was tense, as if it, like a body of work, were on trial. What was there wasn't enough, what might be there was beyond her. She could also be a body of water, affected by an autonomous, distant moon. With tides, not nerves. Her inventiveness was a sponge, and it was rock, scissors and paper, too. She wanted to play, but she didn't know which game. Then she turned on some music and danced. In motion, she produced a funny face. She jumped in the air and sang the lyrics: "I make my bed and I lie in it." She was weird, a character. I'm next to human, she supposed.

In an episode on TV Madame Realism hadn't watched, John Hightower played a poet, an educated man who lived in the

country. The sun beat down on him. The field and he were
parched. He didn't have many lines, and his part wasn't particularly distinguished or profound. Hightower hadn't received
much attention as the poet, a kind of straw man, and even in a
field where he was the only serious artist, he was overlooked. He
took comfort in his uniqueness, he was one of a kind. His agent
told him, you're great, an original. No one acts or interprets
the way you do.

Madame Realism didn't know Hightower.

It was the second summer the Mets won the series. For Joe
Loman it was the single event that made his day, his month, his
year. It pierced the doom and gloom. Loman was more than a fan,
he was a fanatic. He collected cards, autographs, attended every
home game with his season pass. In the next world he wanted to
play first or second base. He wore a Keith Hernandez pin on his
shirt. To earn money Loman was a script doctor and a ghost
writer. He kept his hand on the pulse. Loman was nobody's
dummy. He played his cards close to his vest and suspected
everyone. He didn't work cheap.

Madame Realism didn't know Loman.

She lowered the volume, but she could still hear herself
think. She opened her messy closet. She couldn't throw anything
out. There were shelves, compartments, boxes, drawers. A walk-in
closet big enough to live in. Inevitably, she would be inundated
by stuff, suffocated by the little things in life, submerged under
the weight of kitsch and kultur. Madame Realism couldn't decide
what was trivial, insincere, fake, inauthentic, frivolous, super-
ficial, and gaudy; she herself was all of these. And crude, rude,

stupid, obtuse and mean. And honest, real, prescient, dense, apparent, transparent, smart, and beautiful. In different situations she was different things and to different people she was different people. Reality was a decision she didn't make alone.

(What's real to you isn't to me, she mentioned inadvertently in another story. Madame Realism once found herself in a Guy de Mauppassant tale, the one about a man who picked up a piece of string in the road, and because he did, because he saved things, he had a bad end. One thing led to another, what had seemed a nothing operation—picking up a piece of string in the road—changed the direction of his life. That's because you never know who's watching or what the consequences are. Life and fiction, Madame Realism thought, are a series of incidents and accidents. Everyone faced the possibility of a stupid end or of being stupid to the end.)

Bending down to save something and place it in her messy closet, Madame Realism wondered if one day she would be destroyed or defeated by her own desires and devices. She accumulated. But if she saved everything, there wouldn't be a place for herself. Maybe she could expand, move or change. But most of her changes were minor adjustments. She was set on her ambiguous course.

What Madame Realism didn't treasure affected her as much as what she did.

Somewhere else Hightower's sweating and ranting:

People tell me, "Hightower, you're not capable of being understood. You expect too much." I don't want to talk to these people because they'll tell me their opinions. I'll be forced into comic book situations worse than the one I'm living. That would be death. I'm sick because I'm conscious. I'm important, but I'm not yet considered a genius. Art isn't recognized by everyone, it's not quantifiable or practical. It's for the fine and discerning. Beauty is the basis of quality. How many people do I need to please anyway.

When Hightower finished delivering his impromptu manifesto, which he performed impeccably and with passion, he looked over the field. He was far ahead of everyone, miles ahead, and heads taller. He raced away, aghast, like Hamlet's father's ghost.

Hightower phoned Loman. They were contentious buddies from way back.

Loman's at his computer, ghosting a self-help manual:

You're asking yourself why you get up in the morning; why you go to the same job every day; why you live alone or with the same person even though you're bored out of your mind; you're wondering why life goes on without the great highs you had when you were a teenager. You were miserable then too. But probably you don't remember. You were doing drugs. You remember that you were young and a lot of life wasn't behind you. But don't think about that. That won't help you. That's why you're down. You can't control this stuff once it gets going. Ignore it. Deny it. Just hang out, exercise, be seen, never say die, diet, don't eat fat, don't admit anything, you're not unhappy, get lifted not uplifted, make money not love. Stop complaining.

Meanwhile Madame Realism left her apartment and her closet. She still had a shelf in her mind, where she stored and catalogued experiences and memory, so she felt safe to walk outside. It was a fantastic night. She pretended she could understand other people. When she entered her favorite bar, her neighborhood bar, Madame Realism saw two characters perched on stools in her usual place. Part of her didn't like being displaced, another part invited the unexpected, unanticipated, and unintended. She wanted to do the inviting, though, and the tables were turned. She was a guest.

What Madame Realism didn't apprehend might be more resistant than what she did.

Hightower and Loman were talking and gesturing, their hands and mouths furious implements. Madame Realism had to shove her barstool around and in, but finally she discovered a place at the counter. She wasn't going to let a couple of strangers push her around. She'd adjust, fight, or hold her own, though she wasn't sure what that was.

Unabashedly Madame Realism listened in. She had decided years ago that if she listened only to herself, she'd go crazy.

Loman growled:

You're too subtle, Hightower. You have to reach more people. Appeal to a wider audience. The umpire behind the plate makes calls, instant decisions. Ball, strike, he stands for the people. You think baseball can be played for one person alone? Broaden your base. You can't expect people to get your performance. You have to deliver. Be obvious. What would a baseball game be like if there was only one person in the stands. What if one player ran from base to base, and no one had any expectations about his getting home, or stealing second, sliding over home base or getting a hit. You have to score.

Hightower glowered:

Obvious? An umpire judges baseball. You want him to judge my performance? You think I should respond to, that's a ball, that's a strike? Not everyone in the stands likes the umpire's calls, there's a minority who argues. And some throw beer at each other. There should be a level of civilization, of civilized behavior we agree upon. Let people use dictionaries. Read the work of James Joyce. Everyone should know Shakespeare. There's excellence, standards, otherwise democracy runs amok. Raise the level, don't wallow in it. You pander to the lowest impulses. Broaden my base! Limit your baseness!

Like a wedge between the two, Madame Realism inserted herself. It was characteristic for her to jump in and sink or swim, and sometimes she did both:

You say umpire, he says critic. You say ball game, he says theater. Who chooses the game? the umpire? the critic? Who decides on the players and the rules? I could go on and on.

Loman and Hightower looked at her. Loman thought Madame Realism struck out. She wouldn't even get to first base. Hightower dismissed her. He decided she wasn't very advanced.

Madame Realism went further:

If I were a sonata by Bach, or a song by Courtney Love or Ray Charles, an antique hourglass or a home page on the Web, a china figurine, or a painting by Caravaggio, who decides what I mean? What makes me valuable or lets me be thrown out in the garbage? My projection isn't yours even when you and I go to the same movie.

They ignored her.

Loman raved:

Your purity, Hightower, makes me sick. You wouldn't know what was great if it bled all over you. We're all just pitching balls or strikes. . . .

Hightower reacted:

You want to please everybody, Loman, anybody. You have no eye. No taste. You know nothing of beauty or the spirit that's necessary for seeking truth and creating art.

Loman bellowed:

For values, I go to the marketplace. You don't have an audience, because you don't deserve one. Elitist!

Hightower countered:

You disregard immutable laws that inspire all great endeavors and enduring work. Vulgarian!

Madame Realism wasn't sure what was really at stake. She'd heard it was Western civilization. She displayed her version of the pleasure principle:

I seek pleasure, and I'll do anything to get it. We do any-thing to please ourselves, but we call it other names. Don't doubt that. I can be vicious in the pursuit of my pleasure. I fill my life with beauty, ugliness, happiness, despair, the cheap and the expensive, things are things. I need them, want them, I encounter them, they encounter me. I play them, they play me. We're all left to our own devices.

Madame Realism hated to feel that anything was insignifi-cant. But her performance might be another exercise in futility.

Hightower and Loman couldn't continue to ignore Madame Realism even though she was obscure to both of them. There they were—three characters in a situation together. They came from different places and found themselves sitting on barstools in the same bar. It was a dialogue or a car crash. Any one of them could have been the piece of string, the narrator, or the man who bent down. Any one of them could've been somewhere else or in another position.

Loman slammed his icy mug of Miller High Life on the counter:

> I'm through handling you with kid gloves, Hightower. You'll never be major. Face it. You think you're ahead of everyone, but you've lost the race. You're a loser.

Hightower raised his glass and protested ironically:

> You have a mob mentality, you're trying to satisfy the lowest denominator. You speak down because you haven't an idea in your head. You're just a craven, trendy follower.

Madame Realism threw her drink to the ground. The glass shattered. Give me a break, an epistemolgical break, she declared. She pushed both of them away from her. They were crowding her. I don't have answers, but I need room. Her frustration showed, like a rash all over her body. I don't throw much away. I need to clear a space. You're tired, you're a couple of drunken clichés.

Hightower and Loman objected in unison:

> We aren't clichés. We're being unfairly caricatured.

What Madame Realism couldn't escape was bigger than she was.

Madame Realism reconsidered:

I hear your words. But did you choose them or did they just come to you? I draw and withdraw, I get drawn, and I'm drawn into your argument. I try to keep my eyes open to see you, but I can't stop recognizing you as I do. I didn't organize the bar. I didn't organize your arguments. They've been around a long time. It's beyond my control, but you have become figures of speech. And I'm a condition like you. A piece of circumstantial evidence too.

When Madame Realism came face to face with characters and notions she didn't subscribe to, like a magazine she'd never ordered, she felt surrounded or blocked. Or thrown against a brick wall. Madame Realism sometimes wanted to respond in other ways. She wanted to rid herself of some beliefs, put them away like objects in her closet or toss them out for good, but she was never sure if she did or could. Completely. For one thing, she couldn't even keep track of all her opinions, prejudices, and points of view. They popped up at the weirdest moments. She couldn't always account for them. Worse, she didn't always believe her beliefs. She held some of them like a hand in cards or a script she didn't know she'd been reading. She tried to subject her ideas to analysis, doubt or possible evacuation. But every time she put one aside, or thought she did, another became bigger and moved into the vacancy. She wanted to shake free, but badly conceived and imperfect notions were clinging to her. She could smell them, like a sweet perfume named Sin.

Like sin, one's own history is not original, but it weighs heavy. Madame Realism's history was original only to herself.

Engrained notions were stealthy and resilient. They were permanently dyed into her woolly identity. And since she couldn't easily step outside her own situation or context, it was improbable to ask others to step outside theirs instantly. This was why, she found, most discussions took effect long after they were over. And why she saw things differently later.

Loman bought Madame Realism a drink. She never turned down a free drink, on principle. She had more trouble because of her principles than anything else. And with the drink in her hand, Madame Realism became fully part of this moment or episode. It didn't matter that it might be another déjà vu or received idea. (In some quarters this event might circulate as a joke, a performance or a case of mistaken identity.) Whatever they were, whoever they were, the three of them were relating and in some way equivalent and unequal.

Madame Realism was intoxicated. She couldn't get rid of anything. Her closet was a mess. She could deposit Hightower and Loman in it. She considered bringing them home with her, but she didn't know where'd she'd place them. She might let time settle the argument, since time wasn't necessarily on anyone's side. That might be a solution, she brightened, if time were truly faceless and without envy. But time was also an idea, and it wasn't empty or free of constraints and human engineering. Madame Realism looked at Loman and Hightower. They were still baiting each other.

Madame Realism would never know where to put everything she owned, or collected, or that collected around her. She'd never know where to put everything that happened to her. She'd keep rearranging things.

Madame Realism looked around the smoky room. Stevie Winwood's "Bring Me a Higher Love" was playing on the juke-box, some people were kissing, some playing pool, and others were just staring straight ahead and drinking. Madame Realism's attention settled on the startling array of glasses behind the bartender. Small, large, thin, thick, short, tall, wide, narrow, plain, fancy. All shapes and sizes. If people were containers, she wondered what kind of glass she'd be, what kind of drink. A broad-mouthed Martini, a cool, narrow flute of Champagne, an impatient and short shot of Scotch. Or a mixed drink, a concoction served in a versatile shape. Smiling, Madame Realism bought a round for Hightower, Loman and the bartender.

She looked around the room again. She liked bars, all kinds of them. She thought she always would. They were a part of her. She hoped she'd always enjoy walking into one, taking a seat, seeing the shiny surface of the counter, watching a bartender mix a drink, and listening to strangers talk bar talk. It was a relief to her.

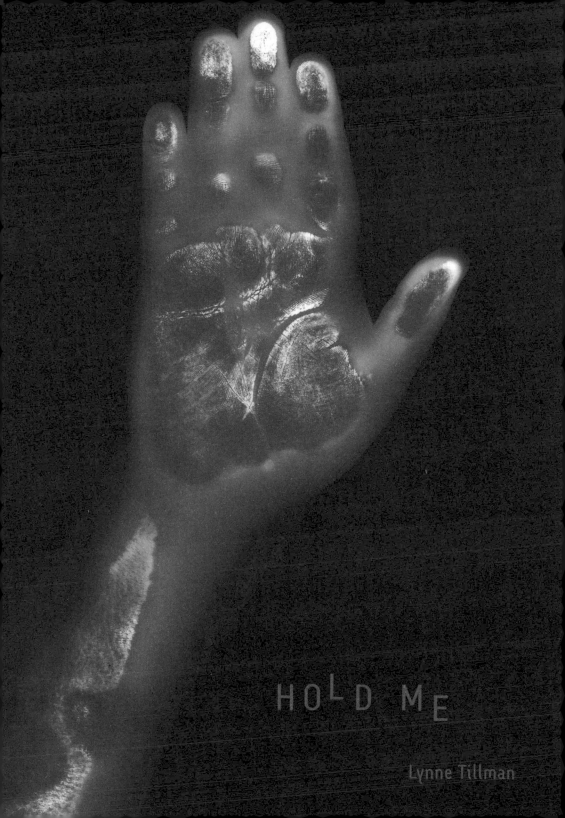

HOLD ME

Lynne Tillman

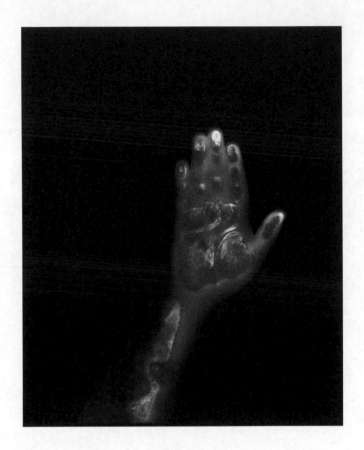

Gary Schneider, CHLOE AT TWO, 1996. Toned gelatin silver print. 8 x 10 inches. Collection of the artist.

HOLD ME
(9 STORIES)

She liked her body when she was a child. Naked, she would look at it in the tall mirror in her parents' bedroom. Then the house was quiet, and she was unique, alone. The house to her was like her body, but it was big and magnanimous and accepted her into it, always. Like a lover, it jealously guarded her from outsiders and kept her to itself.

On those days of solitude, she lay on its cool, naked floor, pressed her face to its wide chest. She pretended her lover was under her, stroking her, caressing her small body, even tracing a path along her spine, fusing top to bottom in sensation. She lay still, quiet as the house, and, full of unrecognizable feeling, she waited.

When the girl heard familiar voices outside, she raced upstairs to her room, whose arms embraced her and made her feel safe. She would, she thought, as she put on her gloves years later, never feel so safe again.

The pensive young woman lifted the scissors from the table and grabbed a bunch of her thick hair. With one motion, she sliced the bunch off. She chopped at the rest, her hair collecting on the floor like discarded thoughts. Rubbing the short, severe hairs on her head, she studied the phone as if it might tell her how she looked. Then she picked up the receiver and punched in a number.

She said: Hi. Listen. Don't say anything, OK? I have to say this. I want quiet the way you do, sure, comfort, but I want things amped, big, things I don't know, I want to go where I've never been. I don't really care about a nice home, I'm not nice. I want privacy. I like being alone. I don't want falling in love, I don't want it. If it runs me, it runs everything. I don't love you. I don't want to love you.

She hung up and cradled the stupid telephone against her chest.

The dental hygienist held the man's jaw and pulled his lip farther from his gum.

"When I was a kid," she said, "every night, I sat at dinner with my parents, and both of them had false teeth, complete sets, and they were only thirty, and the sound of their teeth when they chewed, I hated that sound, you ever hear it?"

He hadn't but he nodded. Her face was too close, intimate as a lover's. Her make up was thick over tiny pimples and large pores.

"So I knew what the future was going to bring," she said.

The hygienist poked a sensitive area. "That's your bad pocket," she reminded him. He winced. The hygienist patted his cheek as an afterthought.

"I knew I'd have to marry a dentist or go into the field."

To friends, he'd described her as the Nazi hygienist, because she loved her work too much.

She persisted at the bad pocket, ripping anxiously at his rotten flesh. Then she paused, to wipe blood from the corners of his mouth, and somehow he started crying. The hygienist nodded, with compassion, he decided, chose a different sharp instrument and went back to work.

E ven last night's dirty dishes looked like rebukes.
    The fragile wine glass slipped from her grip and shattered
to pieces. Last night's grease had congealed on everything,
the plates, cups, fat had separated into ugly units. The tiny glass
splinters presented more domestic dangers. She scrubbed the
pots, urged the fat off forks and knives, and scoured the sink. No
justice, no peace, she thought, restively, and read the label on the
dishwashing liquid. So many little words. Her sister's anger left
her none.

    She picked up a disgustingly clean plate. Maybe she'd smash
it against an innocent wall. She raised her arm and held the pose
too long.

    Instead she went to bed and, like a child, pulled the covers over
her head. She smashed wordless ghosts of things in her dreams.

H
e took a determined breath in the cold room and, naked, pressed his body against a large, picture window. The brilliant fall forest declared itself vital, impressive, and indifferent. He thought he should shave. He traced the contours of his face.

Grieving was the most private act a human being could do, next to shitting, he figured. You could have sex in public more easily than you could shit in public. Grief is shit.

No one had cried, no one in his family broke down, they held on to what they felt, it might expose more than sadness, they kept it in themselves. He listened to his own intake of breath, he watched his mother furtively wipe her eyes, he saw his brother's brow furl like a insignificant ripple in an otherwise placid lake, he watched his father grimace and his arm jerk involuntarily at his side. The gestures commenced a sort of mourning show. He'd never seen their faces like this, stunned silly by life's ultimate weapon.

His grief had no public now. It was when he jerked off and tried to feel good that he let go.

Earlier, what he had said was, You have to take loss, handle it, grab it, just take it. It's your life, you make it what it is. In him, like a drum roll, his words repeated, and as he worked in the garden, digging holes and planting seeds, he felt the world enclose him like an oversized coat. There was no use, no protection, she had answered, and pulled her hat on. She disappeared a little then, tugging at the shapeless hat, tucking unruly hair inside, touching the stiff collar on her coat—and this would not protect her, either. He swallowed, the heat of the day hit him, and then he wiped his brow. His body was mimicking itself, no, other bodies, he decided, and nothing was natural really.

The green ocean spewed dirty foam, the roiling mess spit its way to the shore. The man tensed against the wet, cold air and dropped his shoulders. Then he clenched them and wrapped his black scarf carefully around his neck and under his blue summer jacket. He moved one leg farther from the other and stood with them spread wide apart. He thought, idiotically, I'm facing the ocean. He stuck his chin forward and wondered if he might appear heroic to someone. He looked at the horizon. He smiled at himself, chin jutting into the wind, arms hanging loosely by his sides, a man of a certain age alone on the beach at winter. Nolo Me Tangere, he thought. Then he looked around, saw no one, and slapped himself in the face.

L ove stories are remarkably the same, she said to the guy she secretly loved. He lit her cigarette, nimbly. Then, and she knew he would, because he always did, he tossed his head to the left and glanced at her. He was whimsical today, playful. She noticed, the way she always noticed, how blue his veins were, how uneven the tone of his skin, how ragged his nails. His palms were plump, like the belly of sparrows. His flesh was him, untouchable, ungraspable.

She imagined taking a razor and drawing a line in his soft palm. She imagined blood seeping out, wantonly exposing the stuff inside him, the secret of him, which, like his love, she wouldn't know.

The mother knitted, the son watched MTV, the daughter drifted away, disconsolately tugging at an earring, as if she might remind herself of something that was escaping. In a moment, the mother looked up, awake now to her intense, nuclear world, and pulled bright red yarn from the cloth bag at her feet. How long had she had the bag? As long as they were alive.

The mother had always knit. The staccato of the knitting needles would be how the son brought his mother back, evoked her, long after she was gone—she's going now, the doctor had whispered. The daughter had despised the click clack of the needles, the mother's measured, persistent beat behind her every runaway daydream.

The daughter drifts off and tugs at an earring. Something eludes her. She strains to hear the fitful sound.

The
Lost
City
of
Words

Lynne Tillman

Kiki Smith, Cups and Salver, *1995. Color photograph.*
4 x 6 inches. Collection of the artist. Courtesy of Kiki
Smith and Lynne Tillman.

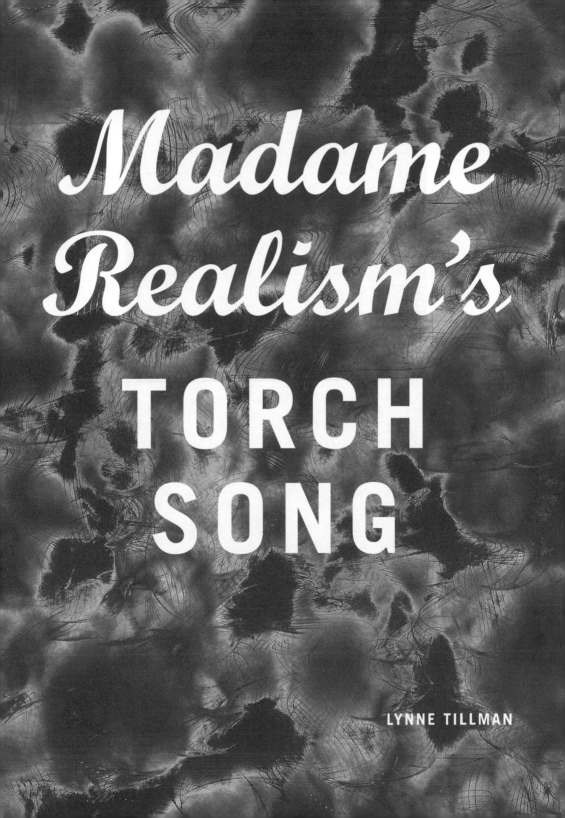

Madame Realism's

TORCH SONG

LYNNE TILLMAN

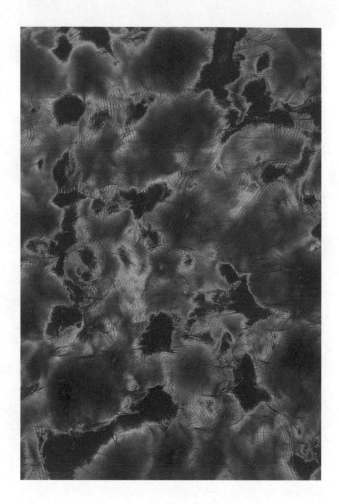

Marco Breuer, Unititled (Heat/Gun), *2001.*
Study for SMTWTFS. *Silver gelatin paper, burned.*
9 x 6 inches. Collection of the artist. Courtesy of
Roth Horowitz.

MADAME REALISM'S TORCH SONG

The other night, as he sat near the fire in Madame Realism's study, in the place where chance had made them neighbors for a period of time, Wiley said: "Things go on we don't know about. They happen in the dark, metaphorically sometimes, but maybe you don't want to talk about dark stuff now."

"Marilyn Manson," Madame Realism said, "told someone on MTV that Lionel Richie was the heart of darkness."

"There's the light side. But it has a shorter life."

Wiley struck a match.

"It sparks, flares, burns, burns out."

He turned from the fireplace, where he was watching the fire, to her. Wiley looked grave or intent. Madame Realism felt strange, the way she often did. She hadn't known him very long, and, for a moment, he spooked her. Then he returned his attention to the hearth.

"Fire's positive, negative, amoral, not capable of reason, which reminds me of something . . ."

"Are you going to tell me a ghost story?" Madame Realism asked.

Wiley's large, almost childlike eyes were a silvery grey, like his hair, but his irises were flecked with brown and yellow, and especially when the fire caught them, they luminesced like a cat's. He stoked the fire, and it leaped higher into the air.

"Do you believe in ghosts?" he asked.

Tonight Wiley's manner or words or tone or bearing bordered on the dramatic. Did she believe in ghosts? She felt ghosted. Ghosts had a place in her vocabulary. Did it matter if they existed? She expected to be haunted by her past, and bodies kept turning up. Wiley might be someone who knew her differently from the way she knew herself, or he might be someone she once knew, disguised. His voice soothed and disquieted her. It was oddly familiar, but then lately everyone seemed familiar, which was a benign kind of horror.

"You and I are sitting together, talking. We came here to get away, and far off, in a place you've never been, or at home, something is happening that could undermine your plans, a lover is slipping out of love, or someone is scheming against you."

Madame Realism noted to herself that she'd found a dire soulmate, another paranoid. Wiley nodded circumspectly or as if he'd heard her thoughts.

"We have very little control, all our small plans can be over-turned in . . ."

He snapped his fingers. It was an old-fashioned gesture. His fingers tapered elegantly at the ends. In another life, he might have been a Flamenco dancer.

"In politics, nothing is really hidden. In your life, if someone moves faster, or decides to play hard ball, or has a scheme and you have a small role, or you're a bystander, or an obstacle, your life changes. We're ants, or tigers, or rats, and we run from one place to another, avoiding or ignoring what's probably inevitable. Something, an enemy, could just . . ."

Wiley tended to finish his sentences with his hands, and this time he moved his left hand in the air, drawing a line through the space in front of him.

Madame Realism focused on the fire, because his eyes were becoming impenetrable, like colored contact lenses. She stared into it, seeing and not seeing, hypnotized or lulled. His words and pauses were the soundtrack to its chemistry.

"But it's important to let things develop, even in the dark, because surprise is like fire—positive and negative. So I like found poems and objects, and this may be crazy, but I make things disappear, just to find them. I study ordinary actions and reactions and all kinds of innocent signs. The collision of uneven things provokes a third element."

Wiley clapped his hands together.

The flames burned indifferently in the fireplace, and Madame Realism thought of alchemy, which usually never came to mind. There was a time, she supposed, when art and science were indivisible and the place where they fused might have been alchemical.

"Do you love fire?" he asked.

"I don't know if I'd call it love."

To herself she proposed: Imagine life without fire. But she couldn't. The world was raw, endless and empty. She got no further.

"I've considered pyromania," she went on, "but I don't know what it'd be in place of, unless there's an infinite parade and you could love millions of different things. Would pyromania substitute for heterosexuality? I could be attracted to men and want to start fires and see them burn, while watching handsome men put them out."

Wiley stared at her now, with open affection. She thought about the true marriage of opposites, attraction wedding repulsion, and a headline: Pyromaniac is a Firefighter.

Earlier she had started the fire that glowed now by twisting single pages of old newspaper into rodlike forms and placing kindling on top of them, arranging the thin sticks of dry wood into a configuration she'd never tried before, but which Wiley had employed, effectively, when Madame Realism first visited him. He was, in his words, "originally a country person, adept at firebuilding." His wife had disappeared two months or years ago, Madame Realism couldn't remember now, and he didn't say more about it or her. He went about building the fire, patiently teaching her his surefire method, which she hadn't yet perfected.

"What matters to me," Wiley said, "is the subtle experiment. It appears insignificant but breeds results no one would expect. Unexpected results from ordinary things are wonderful."

Not unwanted pregnancies, she thought, and poked the fire, which was alive and raised its red-hot head quickly. She always wondered what ordinary was. She always thought she would remember which was the best technique to start a fire, but she didn't. She didn't write anything down; she relied on memory. She didn't like tending a fire; she was easily distracted. She didn't like having to watch it to make sure it kept burning.

"I don't want my illusions to protect me," Wiley said, warming to his subject. "I need to protect them. I have to distinguish between fantasy and evidence, the world outside me. I want to produce fantastic things and control the things I make and do, but I also don't. I'm caught in that drama, a two-hander, but they're my hands, so I'm playing with myself."

The double entendre dropped plumply at her feet. Wiley didn't seem to notice; he was inside his own theater. Madame Realism hesitated.

"I don't want to be manipulated," she said.

It was an ugly word, but she pronounced all its syllables distinctly. Then she added: "But sometimes manipulation is fun. So maybe that's not true."

Tonight the fire caught easily, but she didn't know why. Yesterday she had placed the kindling in approximately the same way, and it hadn't. There was a blazing fire now when yesterday the fire had died out, because of the wetness of the wood or a slight difference in the configuration of the kindling and small logs with which Madame Realism always began or because she had become absorbed in other matters. Maybe she'd forgotten she'd started a fire.

"That's the battle," Wiley said, seemingly out of nowhere or out of no place she was. Was he thinking about manipulation? Or fire?

"What I love most I can't control," Madame Realism said.

Like conversation, the immediacy of it, and how she never knew why it had started, what its necessity was, where it was going to end up or what its lasting effects might be, if any. Conversation was ordinary, but it was also an unforeseeable element that allowed for eruptions in the everyday. Madame Realism saw herself vacillating inside the grid, with other creatures, temporary set pieces on a chess board. She often wanted to leap into the corny unknown. Something about Wiley and his wondrous eyes—Renaissance orbs—encouraged that longing. But escape, she'd been told a million times, was impossible. It also had predictable forms and outcomes.

"In ordinary encounters," he went on, "we expect people to hold up their end of the bargain. If you or I did something strange at dinner, didn't pass the salt, or if you didn't answer a friend's 'how are you?'—something as nothing as that—the whole situation would become tense, people would get angry, and all you'd done was not respond."

Madame Realism considered responses, his and hers, and the fire's. A fire dies out, when it's not tended, not responded to, but it could do the opposite; it could spread rapaciously, but if she were in the room, she'd notice it, because the heat would become overpowering. I'd sense it, she thought, though sometimes when Madame Realism was working or on the telephone, she did not notice something that could, if not checked in time, hurt her. A fire might spread quickly and overcome her. If she didn't escape fast enough, she could be badly burned, maybe suffer grotesque disfiguration, requiring costly surgery to return her face to relative normality—normality is always relative—though not ever again to be pretty or even attractive. Or she might die.

Madame Realism didn't know how much time had passed. A minute. Maybe more. Wiley waited quietly for her to return. His having come from the country implied reserves of patience, to her. But Madame Realism hadn't asked which country. Still, farmers everywhere wait for eggs to hatch, crops to ripen. Wiley seemed an unlikely farmer. She knew little about him; he could be anything. She wondered why his wife had left him, or if she even existed; she wondered if he missed her and still wanted her, if he would forever, no matter what her response to him was now.

When Madame Realism was no longer in love, her lover's eyes, which in the middle of an exacting passion she could not leave, whose every glance she scrutinized to discern greater meaning and which she thought unforgettable, when she was so far from any feelings of love or lust as to make recollection or meaning impossible, her lover's eyes and every other aspect of him lost interest, as if he and they had never been capable of exerting it. Bliss metamorphosed into disgust. In that sense, love was an experiment with unexpected results. Relationships were unpredictable. She had been told, by men, that men were more generous or more practical than women and could easily have sex again with anyone they once loved. She didn't feel she could ask Wiley about that, yet.

He bunched up a sheet of newspaper and placed it nonchalantly near the flames; it might catch if the fire moved its way.

Then he dropped a chocolate-covered cherry into his mouth and straightened its crinkly gold wrapper on the slate floor as if he were ironing it. She liked the smell of clothes being ironed but wasn't sure if she liked that gesture and questioned how much meaning to give it.

"A fire changes all the time," he said, in an ordinary way. Madame Realism now watched it like a movie, whose characters she invented. She sat closer to it, wanting everything in close up. She tried to feel what she believed she was supposed to feel near a fire, heated by its quixotic flames.

The fire changed, but it also stayed the same, a blur of blue purple yellow orange red. Ephemeral, shifting, restless. With just a sheet of newspaper tossed casually onto it, it roared approval and grew bigger. She liked watching it, but it could also become boring, tiresome, the way anything could, especially when you were older and more in need of novelty. Sometimes she found herself feeding it like a child, until she lost interest, which she shouldn't if it were.

Wiley stood up, brushing off his black jeans.

"Do you think about beauty?" he asked.

"Sometimes, but I'm not sure how," she said, feeling a little melancholy, the way she did on her birthday. Beauty was the point, and it was pointless, too.

"Is your ghost story about beauty?" Madame Realism asked.

"Beauty's a ghost that haunts us," Wiley said, comically. Then he hunched his back and extended his arms, spreading them wide like the wings of a bat or an angel.

A figure of loss, she thought.

Together and apart, they looked inward, or at the hearth, and wandered silently into the past. The greedy fire, meanwhile, consumed everything.

"What ghost are you?" Wiley asked, finally.

"Everyone dead I've ever loved."

"Beautiful."

After the fire died, what remained were traces of its former glory, ashes and bits of coal-like wood. Wiley and Madame Realism walked outside, into the cold night. They went in search of shooting stars and other necessary irrelevancies.

Lynne Tillman

the UNDIAGNOSED

Linder Sterling, LINDERLAND AGAINST EVERYONE,
2000. Photographic diptych. Collection of the artist.

THE UNDIAGNOSED

*Boys will be boys /
play with toys /
so be strong with your beast.*
— MICK JAGGER, *MEMO FROM TURNER*

I remember that night. The party was in a ballroom, a magnificent rented room—Le Fin de Siècle—and I was supposed to wear a costume. I wore my father's clothes. He was dead, so I came as any dead man or my father's ghost. Hamlet's father's ghost manifested Hamlet's desire; but I didn't imagine my father whispered to me, I didn't imagine a murder had to be avenged.

No one at the party knew what man I was, and, like so much of life, it was only in my head. Costumed, I felt I could not be myself, which had obscure benefits.

The ballroom was decorated with streamers and flowers, tiny incandescent lights trailing the walls, larger globes attached to the high ceiling, then more tiny lights running the length of it. I hated the room's having been rented, as if grandness could be, intimating that all my pleasures were temporary and, worse, for sale.

Small lamps shaped like flames lit the requisite white cloaked tables. The flames twinkled on and off, inflecting the partygoers' faces with unintended seriousness or grotesqueness, They couldn't see themselves, how unholy shadows created other masks on their faces and marked them as tormented or angry. Visible to themselves, they might have been dismayed or thrilled. Some lust after distortion. But the unintended is frightening. It illuminates what schemes never do and becomes more indelible than anything that could have been made up or that people could have made themselves into. Accidents and mistakes, like an end game or a tragic virus, carry eternal consequences.

I am consumed by consequences, layered with them.

There was a long table heavy with food, another with wine, another hard liquor, another dark desserts. By the time I arrived—late, I hadn't wanted to show up—people were sated or acquiescent. Some were loonily high or indifferent; the drugs were available in a ridiculous bathroom. Some masqueraders were nearly rigid, or hoping to feel anything, and some were playing a game of promiscuity called choice.

A man dressed as a fool leaped in front of me and screamed, Are you happy? Another, dressed as a rose, exposed his penis to three men—his penis was a thorn in his side. Four women, parading as witches, laughed hysterically. I dislike women who dress up as witches. They are low minded and unimaginative.

I wiggled uncomfortably inside my father's suit. I didn't want to think of his body. I remembered the long, dark hairs on his forearms, the hairlessness of his upper arms and chest, his hazel, illegible eyes, his uneven, uncontrollable mouth, his penis when he urinated, and dressed as a man, I began thinking about men I'd known, and wondered casually, noticing other costumed miscreants and misfits, if I could remember every one of them who mattered to me, and even those who hadn't and didn't at the time when time was unimportant, and if I could see them in my mind's eye and reckon with their foreign, familiar bodies, their alien, similar lives. I'd been raised as a woman. I didn't feel I was one, and I didn't care that I didn't. I didn't know how men felt, what instantly occurred to them, raised as they were, with other postures imposed and other awarenesses impressed upon them. I watched movies about men, I read books. I had sex with them and hung out with them. I had men friends and enemies. I knew men as plumbers, theorists, hairdressers, scholars, bartenders, teachers, lovers, translators, butchers, artists, carpenters, musicians, landlords, actors, paupers, writers, dentists, shoemakers. (Dentists arouse my sympathy, and I particularly like shoemakers.)

I knew men who had no trouble being men, I knew men who were dubious about being men, I knew men who wanted to be women, I knew men who hated women, and those who relished them like succulent meals, I knew men who loved men, I knew men whose best friends were women, I knew men whose fear of vaginas vanquished them (they couldn't go through tunnels), and men who couldn't piss in men's rooms. I knew men who had sex in subway toilets, men who were celibate, men who hated sports, hated books, had eating problems, who hated life, and I knew men who hated how much they needed women, and others who turned their backs on them. I knew men who were depressed and men who were never unhappy (those blessed few). I knew men who were affectionate, lusty, friendly, remote, stupid, tender, courteous, shallow, sexy, cerebral, bold, cowardly, crude, pretentious, kind, and on and on.

I won't go on.

I couldn't remember them all, there were too many. And dressed as a man especially, I felt I knew nothing about them as men. Men qua men, I mused to myself, watching people dance and eat. I also knew little about women, in the same way, being a flawed one, having rejected or scorned what being a woman supposedly entailed. No child? No man? No food? Anyway, the categories were too general, sweeping in their assumptions, and I resist cultural imperatives and operate inside them.

The door opened, and Clint Eastwood entered. He cast a long, romantic shadow. He was rugged, too, as magnificent and big as the space where he was now temporarily installed like a tower. Not the Martello Tower, not Pisa, Watts, not the Texas Schoolbook Depository in Dealey Plaza, but a tall, lean man, who seemed he would never fall, like the Twin Towers.

I wasn't surprised to see him, I'd been expecting him for years. Sometimes I conjured him after watching one of his movies and then in dreams I knew him intimately. Dreams, the mind's gifts, can be sweeter than anything reality offers, and they satisfy me more than sex. Or, they are sex.

Usually when I think about someone, he or she eventually turns up. In a train station, in a bookstore, crossing an alley, around a corner, that face presents itself, stamped onto the present like postage. I have sometimes thought, overdue postage.

Now Clint was here. I was happy, maybe relieved.

The way I remember it, I strode, as best I could, awkward in my father's suit, across the floor toward him. I was trying to imitate a man's gait. Do they throw their shoulders forward more than putative women? Clint was engaged in a subdued kind of shoot out. He couldn't help himself, or the other men couldn't help themselves. Their faces were shot through, anyway, irradiated with alarm and fear; maybe they were just stunned. Clint stood near, and they were dwarfed and dimmed by his cinematic luminosity. Stars do shine, and the men's faces registered that fact, also that Clint had taken the thin cigar from his mouth, after he had rolled it around his lips several times, the way he does in Sergio Leone movies, which usually means something bad will happen or some decisive move will be made.

(I was, I discovered, in a state of amazement, so close to my hero, when I don't have a hero, almost incoherent, and my suit felt even more uncomfortable.)

Clint was rock steady. I thrilled to his stillness, the way he held the world inside him. Silent, contained, he was unsettling as a nature morte. Decisiveness itself is still, like death. And he was, for me, a picture of a man. Maybe the main picture I had in mind against which what were called men were measured, in subtle and obvious ways.

Clint is not like my friend Hamlet. The dear, antagonistic hero acted unmanly, Ophelia and Gertrude growing out of him like branches from a tree. Hamlet had to punish and sever them, or betray his femininity. Their hateful womanishness, their weakness, that baleful susceptibility was only to himself and to other men. Nothing but men.

I thought, suddenly, men must really suffer an awful anxiety of influence. The father's ghost does linger and loom, it must threaten to suffocate them. I noticed some costumed men in the room jockeying for position, and I fit them into this idea.

My neurotic father's suit felt like a prison. But I didn't want to kill him, even if it's the murder I might be forced to commit, later. I could be forced to duel him, when I get around to experiencing my masculinity more fully. I took fencing in college, I remembered.

En garde, ghost.

Look at Clint, I remonstrated to myself, see how he doesn't lean or buckle. But the suit, and a duel, these entrapments didn't fit me. I felt extreme and silly. I wanted to slap my face. Electrifying music heightened all my responses. I was as reactive as a hive. My heart pumped, an ecstatic organ played by Brother Jack McDuff or Jimmy Smith. I needed the soundtrack, a background score, and whatever was playing, whoever the DJ was who moved time along, or kept events in time, I was glad of it. I had lost track.

I took a breath, to steady myself, and shut my eyes. With the beat, I opened them and studied the masqueraders coolly again, especially the men, when I could discern them. It was hard to maintain a distance. Each was dressed as someone he wanted to be or someone he didn't want to be, so he demonstrated a remarkable and aggressive display of self-love or hatred, enacting "I am this," "I am not this." A short, skinny man strutted as a wrestler, a tall, fat one flailed his apron—a rude housewife.

I became a restive, captive character to their ambivalence. I understood it and abhorred it, also, since unrelenting duality infuses everything I do. Every act, too, is against my limits. The body, the first limit. I try to control it, tame it, inflict pain on it, pamper it, release it, wrest it from its history or its shape. I have attempted to abandon it, gorge it, starve it, scar it, mask it, disgrace it, take pride in it, humiliate it, and disown it. But I awoke in it each morning. Still, I didn't envy those who surgically tailored themselves into different bodies. I wouldn't even pierce an ear.

I bet Clint likes his body, I thought, I bet he likes his sharp features, the cool set of his face, I bet he was often embarrassed by how handsome he was. Aging now, he had bravely exposed his flaccid chest, and even so I couldn't forget him as a young man.

The man with no name.

I wasn't his type, not the kind he married or mated with, who looked like the same woman each time, which has a certain economy—men don't have to abandon their mothers, really. But as a man, I thought, maybe he'd like me. I puzzled over this funny notion and wandered away from him.

I like to sit alone, I always have, at parties. I took a seat on a long, crimson, silk couch. Silk doesn't wear well, and it was another sign that the night, and other things, would not last. Dressed as a man, I might incite the notice of disguised strangers who would tell me things I'd never heard and hadn't bargained for. Maybe Clint would come over, if I didn't bother him.

He was glorious across the magnificent, rented ballroom, spotlighted and standing beside a woman dressed up as Andy Warhol—right wig, shock white powdered face. Late Warhol. Clint was showing her his boots, and others were clustered around him, hopefully. Now he looked up, with a wry, exaltant expression, and in that instant, I caught his eye. Maybe I looked like someone he once knew. He bent down again, showing the group the special stitching and tooling, and then nodded, waved or motioned to me. I returned his nod. I distinctly recall the vertebrae of my neck clicking in anticipation.

Clint strode across the shiny black floor, the way I wished I could have.

Once he was beside me, I didn't know what to say. He was silent, too, but that was characteristic of him.

Finally I told him I was wearing my father's clothes.

You're imposturing your father? he asked.

Sort of.

Sort of? he asked.

My father was a difficult man to know. I'm not sure if men are different from women in any interesting way.

Men want sex, settle for money, comfort, mostly everyone settles. What do you want to know?

Whatever you can tell me, I answered.

Clint told me about his father, his father had once dug a hole in the ground, a large hole, no, a pit, and lived in it, as a protest, for a week. He pissed and shit there—he ate ants. Right in the backyard. His father was an ordinary man, a businessman in a small town. But his life, Clint said, depended on his proving he could do this. It was about his manlihood.

Had it been challenged? I wondered.

Had he been in a war?

Did he want his mother?

Is anyone ordinary?

To Clint, I asked, How did his living in a hole affect you?

Well, he said, I've never really thought about it.

Two apache dancers—male and female—raced across the floor. The male lifted the female and sent her crashing to the ground. Then the female lifted the male and did the same.

Equal opportunity, Clint remarked.

Both of us stared, and I thought of animals, horses especially, being broken.

Three people of indeterminate sex strolled across the floor, wearing sandwich boards: He-Male, She-Male, E-Male.

It's not a good time to be a man, Clint said, looking at my suit. He turned the collar up and then turned it down.

Being a woman doesn't appeal much, either. Both positions defy me, in any case, I explained.

Clint said he was uncomfortable with pre-arranged affiliations, and I said, I didn't feel patriotic to a sex. I appreciated the animal in me, I said, but felt I had no nature, certainly no great love of it, so any nature in me was second nature. In all things I just wanted to do what I wanted, without resistance from others, without unnecessary conflict. Life's object was to get as much pleasure as possible or to avoid pain. I took that to heart and let the notion guide me.

We were silent for a bit then, in our own kind of Western, I realized, at least philosophically, and while I pondered my own speech, or outburst, he seemed to chew it over, too.

He told me he hated violence but was also drawn to it.

I told him I loved *Unforgiven.*

He became embarrassed. I wanted to touch his face as if it were a computer screen.

I must be drawn to violence, too, since I enjoy your movies, I went on.

What about *Tightrope?* he asked. The later ones—not the spaghettis. . . .

You're not renouncing those are you?

I don't turn my back on the past, he said.

Only the women? I asked.

Clint looked a little angry then. I worried I'd alienated him. But he just stretched and squinted, his eyes disappearing into thin folds of tanned flesh.

I had to ask him.

Are you afraid to die? I said.

Nope, he said. When your time comes, it comes.

Do you really feel that?

Yes.

Because Westerns are all about death, that's why I asked.

Oh, well, he said, if you put it like that. . . . But I'm not.

Unforgiven is about that.

It's about killing, he said.

Death, I said.

We can stop killing, we can't stop death.

Clint astonished me.

In that instant, I felt I was married to him. And that night, while I watched men and women cavort and sulk, flirt and look dejected, though I felt like an observer, the way I usually do, I felt I was looking for something, too, not just at something. With Clint next to me—we sat this way for the rest of the evening, talking and not talking—and in my father's suit, sometimes forgetting I was wearing it, I thought, I don't look like my father, I'm looking for my father. (I didn't say this to Clint.) And when I find him, I'm going to have to slay him, as in days of yore.

I couldn't believe I thought that. Maybe I didn't. I know I'll never find him.

Later, when Clint left me, to return to the adoration of others, or to being himself, whoever that was, if he could ever be himself, what I wanted to do was go to the movies. I wanted to watch his movies, the early ones. I wanted him like that, then and always.

THRILLED TO DEATH

LYNNE TILLMAN

Jessica Stockholder, YourSkinInThisWeatherBourneEye-
Threads&SwollenPerfume *(detail view from installation at Dia
Center for the Arts, New York), 1995. Courtesy of Gorney Bravin
+ Lee, New York.*

THRILLED TO DEATH

What makes people insecure is when they feel like they're lost in the fun house.

—President Bill Clinton

Because carnivalistic life is life drawn out of its usual rut, it is to some extent "life turned inside out, ... the reverse side of the world." In antiquity parody was inseparably linked to a carnival sense of the world. Parodying is the creation of a decrowning double; it is the same "world turned inside out." For this reason parody is ambivalent.

—Mikhail Bakhtin

It is not only happiness that gives value to life.

—Colette

ONCE UPON A TIME

R ose Hall was riding backward on a train. She was alone.
She felt as free as she would ever be. A man across the aisle
had fallen asleep, and his head had dropped to the side of
his body. His full lips were open and parted, like a fish mouth on
a hook. She watched him, drank beer, and looked at the landscape
pass by dyslexically. Earlier she had wanted to have many lovers
and a large glass of vodka. She wanted everything fast, without
problems or fuss. She laughed at her fantasy of no-fuss love, and
then she didn't. Even earlier she became furious at an elderly
woman who barged in front of her on line. Rose Hall kept silent.
She even bit her tongue. She stared out the window and nursed
her wounds. It was strange how one thing didn't follow another.

Steve Whitehurst saw a man standing in front of a door. The man
was holding a large pot. It appeared to have nothing in it. The
street was dark and the man with the pot was in shadow. Steve
crossed to the other side. He didn't want to get hit on the head.
Protecting his head was weird, he thought, it probably wasn't
worth it. He bought a quart of milk and returned home. He
intended to take his regular route, if the freak with the pot had
disappeared. But he was still standing there, holding the pot.
Steve walked several blocks out of his way, past the Italian Boys
Social Club. They were hopeful Mafia lieutenants. He was used
to them. But the man with the pot set off an alarm. What in hell
was he doing? Steve Whitehurst looked around sharply and put
his key in the door.

Lily Lee Wallner kicked a stone on the sidewalk and watched it hurtle into the gutter. She had few defenses against flagrant beauty, her own impatience, and the strangeness of daily life. She was impatient with life. She succumbed to pleasure when she could. "I submitted, I gave in," she told a friend. "I was enthralled. I was on thrill." She fed her fantasies as if they were hungry. The sky was a bright plastic blue. Almost transparent. Lily Lee walked into the park, to the dog run. She stood there a long time. The dogs greeted each other or didn't, they sniffed each other or didn't. Small catlike dogs pursued unlikely big dogs. The freedom of dogs was beguiling, and Lily Lee liked to imagine an animal's liberty. She walked away, toward the playground, a fortress encircled by rough-hewn, pale blue walls. Children slid down the slides and screamed with savage pleasure. Worried mothers frowned, and patient fathers and happy mothers smiled. Lily Lee didn't want children. She wanted a dog. Maybe that was a fantasy.

Paige Turner wrote in her notebook: "You've never been a child, or you're always a child. Or there is no childhood, or children are innocent, or they're evil, or children and adults have nothing to do with each other, or they have everything to do with each other, they are each other, or how do you stop being a child—at an event? with a recognition? and when, oh when, does childhood end? and when does being alive stop being only colors, smells, and sounds.

"You're little, you're lying in the dark, and you can barely see but you hear noises, voices. Sounds become words, you put two and two together, two words, two sentences, an explanation, everything's explained to you, you're told about the world, you overhear, you pay attention, drink in, you grow bigger, you make up your own stories, you imagine, things happen to you that you can't control, you make your way or you don't. . . ."

Paige washed her hair. It was long, curly, and red. She'd heard jokes about redheads her whole life. She was sick to death of them, she hated being called "Red." Everyone said her hair was her best feature. Maybe she'd bleach it silver. I have a redhead's temper, she noted wryly to herself. Then she laughed out loud.

It was way past her bedtime. Jeff Brown read *Cinderella* to his four-year-old daughter, Kelly.

"Once upon a time, a wealthy man's wife died suddenly. The stricken man mourned her extravagantly. But luckily he had one daughter he adored. Cinderella was kind, bright, and beautiful, like his dead wife. But he was lonely, and he wanted to make a new home for them. So he remarried. Now his new wife also had children, two daughters from a marriage that ended with death. But theirs had not been a happy union, and years of strife had hardened the woman and her daughters. They were blind to anything but their own needs. One could say that she and her daughters were cut from the same loveless cloth, and loving didn't come easily to them and they weren't easily made happy. In her way, the new wife loved her new husband. But it had been a long time since she'd been loving. She guarded her good feelings jealously, as if they could be stolen from her like her wallet. Right after the marriage, the new wife turned against her stepdaughter. Cinderella didn't like her, either. She was ordered to do menial chores and given no time to read stories, which she loved. Her stepsisters passed their days playing games, doing puzzles, studying, and trying on clothes. Cinderella didn't complain to her father, even though she wanted to. She had a lot of pride, but oddly enough, to her annoyance, her father seemed happy with his new wife. . . ."

Kelly's eyes started to close. Jeff watched her face expectantly. Her eyes opened again, and she pleaded buoyantly, Daddy, read more, Daddy, read.

"So day after day, she did the dirty work, pretending it didn't bother her. Night after night, she sat by the fireplace, in a corner of the hearth, surrounded by ashes. She watched the hot fire burn orange and red, then die. She tried not to feel sorry for herself.

"Her dirty face and hands, and soiled, torn clothes, were a constant shame to her. She felt older than her years. Her stepsisters teased her and called her Cindy, because she sat by the cinders. Cinderella controlled her temper. Her face grew masklike, and she never laughed. But, however she felt about herself, she was pretty in her sisters' eyes, and they saw how their stepfather looked at her. Cinderella hadn't planned to make them suffer by comparison, but they did."

Kelly's eyelids dropped and shut tight, and Jeff, tired, jumped to the end of the tale.

"The shoe fairly flew out of the Prince's hand—or so it is said—onto her foot, making a bond with it. The sisters were astonished. So was the Prince. They were even more astonished when Cinderella pulled from her pocket the second slipper and placed it on her other foot. (She did this with a little satisfaction; she wasn't absolutely selfless or a fool.) With the second shoe on, her godmother appeared. She waved her wand over Cinderella, who was transformed again. This time, even more magnificently. Awestruck, the Prince asked her to marry him.

"Now, this is what everyone still talks about. Though she loved the Prince, and accepted his offer, what pleased Cinderella most was her sisters' change of heart. They were ashamed of their behavior and really sorry they'd been so horrible to her. And Cinderella forgave them and said she would always love them. Then she invited them to live with her in the palace. A few days later, when she and the Prince married, Cinderella introduced her sisters to two eligible bachelors. Immediately they fell in love. This made her stepmother proud, even repentant. And, though everything happened very fast, after many years, they are all still together. And so it may be said that they are living happily ever after."

By the time Jeff recited the words "happily ever after," Kelly was lost to sleep. She looked so vulnerable, he wanted to cry.

In the Brothers Grimm version, the stepsisters' eyes are plucked out by doves. "And so for their wickedness and falseness they were punished with blindness for the rest of their days." He didn't want Kelly to hear that. Jeff Brown and his white wife had recently divorced. The truth was, she left him for another man. Jeff resisted his own ugly feelings and they parted more or less amicably. Jeff was a reasonable man. But ever since the divorce, their daughter Kelly had had bad dreams.

Jeff discussed the Grimm version of *Cinderella* with his law partner, Rose Hall. He told her how bloody and cruel it was. It's wild, Jeff said, no matter what version you read, *Cinderella's* a divorce story, right from line one. Then, looking out the window, he said, I want to protect Kelly, but in this world you're a fool, living a fantasy.

Frank Green took life as it came. He prided himself on that. But he envied other people their illusions, their delusions, their dreams. He wasn't a dreamer. He wasn't like that. Plain food, plain living, he wasn't going to kid himself. He had his one chance in life, and if he blew it, that was that. He probably had blown it. But he wasn't a crybaby. He didn't care what other people thought about him.

Frank had a dream. He told his girlfriend, Lily Lee: I'm trapped in an apartment. I'm trapped in a kitchen, it's yellow. I hear a noise. Someone has gotten in. Someone wants to kill me. I see who it is. This person wants me dead, but I can't believe it. I wake up. I have to piss like a racehorse.

A yellow kitchen? Lily Lee repeated, with a wan smile. I'm the kitchen? Frank told her she was being a jerk. "I had to piss, that's all." And then he teased her the way he always did: "You're just half-Chinese."

When it was late at night or early in the morning and the city was silent—like the Tombs, Frank always put it—he opened up to Lily Lee:

"A couple of years ago I felt like, who gives a shit. I hated it, life. Hated myself. I was apathetic. I hated life. Then I wanted to get high all the time. As much of the time as I could. I wanted to feel alive all the time. I drank like a maniac, I went on benders, I caroused with the guys, got stupid, and that started to interfere with the job. I got sloppy. And then I thought about sex all the time. Sex and more sex. I wanted to feel alive. This is before I met you. But the sex was nuts-and-bolts stuff, mechanical. I made up scenes to get myself off. But I had to work at it. I couldn't get off even on my own sexual numbers. It was pathetic. I looked at nuns, I mean, I'm a Catholic, I should be able to, and even school-girls, in their uniforms, but it didn't work for me. I couldn't picture it. I can't get excited if I can't picture it. Then I watched porn all the time. But it made me sad. I don't get off on other people's fantasies."

Lily Lee sighed. She said, I know what you mean. Frank Green was a cop. He fascinated her. They'd met at the hospital where she worked as a nightshift nurse. To Lily Lee he was Paul Newman in Fort Apache, The Bronx. They turned on the TV.

Lily Lee had a dream: A man's following me. I escape wearing heels but I'm in my nurse's uniform. There's blood on it. On the road outside the house, I start walking and hitch a ride with a man on skis. I close my eyes and don't see how fast or where we're going. Then I realize I'm holding on and we're going uphill climbing the Empire State Building—no, the Eiffel Tower. Then I wake up and there's snow and ice. I hang on to his body, my arms around his waist. At first I'm afraid, then I realize I can ski.

Lily Lee put on her blades and skated around the city. She didn't tell anyone about her nightmare. It disappeared with the day. That afternoon she met Frank, and they went to the carnival. They wanted to see "Bonnie and Clyde's Death Car," but they didn't know if it'd be there. Frank told her that when he was a kid, there were real freaks in carnivals. Now, he complained, the sideshow's on the street. Lily Lee grinned and told him to shut up.

THE OMNIPRESENT TENSE

The scene overpowers Paige. She's excitable. She thinks, I'm such a cheap date, maybe I have a cheap date with fate. The carnival gates are wide open. Everyone's been invited by an imaginary host. There's no one to thank or to be grateful to. The chaotic and tacky splendor is disinterested, like a neutral party. All are welcome. Paige likes that.

The carnival seduces Paige the way it always does, ever since she was a kid. It's a phantasm, a phantasmagoric suite of sights. Anything can happen. A carnival was her first taste of sweet earthly danger. She remembers it like her first real kiss, even though the first carnival was just a bunch of tents and displays, games and food, cotton candy, nothing elaborate. But one day it appeared, out of nowhere, in a vacant parking lot, at the end of the block. Strangers lounged on the sidewalk, men with moustaches and muscles, women with red lips and muscles. The grifters seduced the suckers. The short con artists, small time and hapless, schemed and entrapped. The carney kids seemed to have possibilities she'd never know. They ran wild, her mother said.

She was scared of the place and attracted to it. A dark, handsome teenager, years older than her, smiled at Paige, and an unknown thrill curled up her spine.

She's still scared on the rides, thrilled to death.

"And mammoth, now-extinct animals roamed the land, and our ancestors, prehistoric humans, crawled on all fours, on hairy limbs. They didn't have tools or fire. Foliage blanketed the ground. Forests and mountains and lakes and oceans and rivers and valleys were mighty. The hot yellow sun and the cool silver moon and the white nighttime stars generated life, and there was no time. The strange, naturally occurring objects made the world for the creatures below them. They determined the activity of all the incipient or simple humans and the large and small creatures."

Jeff, Rose, and Kelly sit in the darkened theater. The voice-over rolls along as dinosaurs, winged mammals, pterodactyls, and hunched over, crawling, or standing early humans move like ghosts across the 3-D screen. Kelly is a butterfly mounted on her seat. Jeff considers the magnitude of prehistory, first as myth, then as fact. He thinks about evolution, those first human baby steps, the laborious move to stand upright, creatures crawling out of the water onto land and adapting. He wonders if humans are still adapting or if humans are finished, soon to be extinct. He looks at Kelly. She fills him with hope.

Rose has her own hopes. Maybe a life in the country or a life with Jeff, though that might be a bad idea, just a fantasy, and then there's mixing business with pleasure, but none of those rules really matter to her, deep down. Jeff wonders if Rose's in love with him. His wife used to say that, but he thought she was just giving him grief. Rose thinks maybe she loves Jeff. Kelly doesn't like Rose. She wants her mommy and daddy to be together again. Actually, she wants her daddy all to herself.

In the darkened theater, all three discover that wearing 3-D glasses is uncomfortable. Rose is disoriented, agitated. She can't shake an uneasy feeling. Then the show's over and they walk outside. The bright sun hurts Jeff's eyes. Rose squints too. Kelly asks, Daddy, Daddy, go carousel?

Paige wanders through the sprawling carnival, the playground— massive tents, quaint, small buildings, golden facades, enormous terrifying rides, food booths, staged acts, video and computer games, interactive gothic houses of horror. Waves of brilliant color rise and splash over her. A tide of electricity carries her away from shore, from herself. Startling neon signs glare and blink naughtily. Light encases her as if it were a gaudy gown.

Paige strolls slowly up one ramp and then down another, she follows the twists and turns of the road. She's in a labyrinth. She wants to absorb everything. She doesn't want to know where she is. She doesn't want to be herself. Unconsciously she smells perfumes and underarms and hair spray and young and old bodies. The smells of food are memory ridden. Smell is the sense closest to the center of memory in the brain, a psychologist once told her. Even when Paige doesn't remember what is evoked by a scent or aroma, the smell lingers, tantalizingly. Paige believes memory is in every cell of her body.

264   *This is Not It*

Steve Whitehurst sees Paige Turner. Her long, curly red hair. He's always had a thing for redheads. Steve notices Paige while standing behind his uncle's shooting gallery; it's one of his uncle's concessions. Steve wonders if she'll come to his booth. He sets his mind to it, to drawing her closer to the theater of rifles. But she walks away, toward the fortune teller. A couple of black kids pick up rifles. Steve tells them, You have to pay first. One says they don't have money. Steve nods, OK, and they go ahead. But just one round, he cautions. Steve hopes his uncle doesn't spot him doing this. Everyone in his family is in the carney business. Steve's not made for the life.

Grotesque advertisements for horror fan Paige's spirits. I have no soul, she whispers to no one. And I don't want one. But I want something. Maybe I'll run away and join the carnival, call myself Dahlia and paint myself purple, I'll think purple thoughts, and be the purple lady in the sideshow. She wonders if, without the idea of a soul, she can think about beauty lasting, or of anything lasting, of goodness living on after death, of anything of her continuing, or of anything at all in her, or anything that might survive the death of her body. She didn't want the thoughts. A friend told her that's why people have children.

Paige is transfixed by the swirl and rage of the raucous action around her. No one has planned it all, it's not plotted, it's not a plot. She can do whatever she wants. But Paige sometimes finds it hard to choose.

The shocking pink-striped facade of the fortune teller—The Cabinet of Dr. Joy—entices Paige. A poster picture of the fortune teller is dramatic. He's an old man with a white beard and wire-rimmed glasses. He looks serious, Paige thinks, as she takes the plunge and parts the heavy curtains. Though Paige doesn't believe in it, she always has her fortune told. Cards, tarot, palm readings, tea leaves, handwriting, crystal balls. The old man doesn't work that way.

Frank and Lily Lee are riding on the Wonder Wheel. It stops. They're stuck at the top. Frank cracks a joke about there being room at the top for the likes of them. He calls himself legal lowlife. Lily Lee tells him to stop ragging on himself. The little carriage shakes back and forth. Frank takes Lily Lee's hand. I have a secret, he says soberly. Lily Lee looks at him hopefully. You can't tell anyone, he goes on. Only my partner knows, and he's a tomb. Lily Lee listens, waits breathlessly. I murdered a guy, Frank says. They're both silent, the little carriage jolts back and forth. In the line of duty? Lily Lee asks. No, he says, not in the line of duty. I was a kid. It was an accident. They are on top of the Wonder Wheel a long time. Frank stares ahead. He's not frightened. Lily Lee is, but Frank's stoicism infects her. Frank asks, Do you think you could marry a man like me? Lily Lee swallows and coughs nervously. Is he serious? Frank goads her, But since you're half inscrutable, I'll never know what the real deal is . . . Lily Lee bites her tongue. She says, If you keep on this half business. Then she breathes in and out. I know my mother's family will love you, anyway. So that's a yes, Frank says. If we live, Lily Lee answers, looking down, her heart in her mouth.

Paige Turner instantly and inexplicably comes under the spell of the fortune teller. A charming mind reader, she decides. The fortune teller stares calmly at Paige. He takes her into his inner sanctum. He motions that she sit down. He wants to hypnotize her. Does she mind? When he looks at her with his peculiarly intense eyes, she says, No, go ahead. Then she adds, What have I got to lose? Your inhibitions, he answers serenely. But he continues, I don't predict the future. You don't? Paige asks. No, he says, I predict the past. Predict the past? Paige repeats. He dangles a silver object in front of her eyes and speaks in a warm voice and her eyelids grow heavy, as he says they will.

Steve Whitehurst's uncle returns and tells him to take tickets at the sideshow. That's more your line, he adds, to Steve's annoyance. In an uncanny way, his uncle's right. He's more at home in front of the Odditorium than behind a counter where people shoot at targets with ugly brown rifles. The Odditorium is out of date, the name was used a long time ago, but the sideshow business—there's no business like the sideshow business—is having a comeback, he reassures himself. Steve walks over to the ticket booth. He doesn't really like the current freaks who are bringing sideshows back, but at least they don't want the life to disappear. We're up against soap operas and daytime talk shows, his uncle complained all the time, freaking talk shows, freaks for free, but they're just talk, blah blah. People come because they still want the real thing, live stuff, live exhibits.

But not as much as they once did, Steve knows. He smiles at the posters around him, relieves the other guy in the booth, and remembers the redhead nearby. Live exhibits, Steve thinks.

Nothing dies here, everything's alive, vital, the old man chants. You're in a carnival. You're in the funhouse. But it's not a funhouse. It's also a tragic place, a cemetery for things that aren't dead. A home for the hidden, the driven, the obscene, and sometimes something leaps out, but it's not what it seems. What arrives wears a costume, and an event is a mask. It may be something else. It may be light or dark and really be its opposite. But there are no simple opposites.

Paige, you will encounter your contrariness and bare it boldly. Your ambivalence will concoct dreams beyond your wildest wishes. Here, your contradictions may be honeyed and bitter.

Paige tastes bittersweet chocolate in her mouth.

Paige, here you can be anything. Where are you now?

Paige listens to something, maybe it's the fortune teller: Where are you?

I don't know. I can't tell.

Do you see a window?

Yes, I see it.

Go through it. What do you see now?

Ropes, funny china, people in costumes, neon lights, monkeys on trees, crates of fruit, my mother, a stack of orange books, and so many colors, and there are three ways to go, paths. . . .

Take one.

Where am I? Paige asks herself. This is corny. Maybe I'm having a near-death experience.

Where am I? she asks aloud.

You are not yet. You are not I.

I know that. I don't want to choose a path.

Then you'll stand in one place.

I'm at a standstill, Paige thinks. How did the fortune teller know?

Jeff Brown carries Kelly. She's a drowsy bundle in his arms. Rose and Jeff walk to the sideshow. Signs proclaim exhibits and acts— a bearded lady, a tattooed man, a sword swallower, the largest rat in captivity. I don't want to see a giant rat, Rose announces, disgusted. Her lip curls. Jeff hates that. And as her lip curls, and she says this, an amplified voice blurts: See the incredible rat. Come, look at the largest rat in captivity. Look at the giant rat. They see a poster for a hunger artist. That, I have to see that, Rose says. They pay their money to Steve Whitehurst. Jeff's glad Kelly's asleep.

They enter a room and pass the giant rat in a glass case. Rose ignores it. There's another glass cage with hefty cockroaches and, in its own separate section, a furry tarantula. A man-eating snake rests, coiled, in its box. Then they approach the hunger artist. She is a woman in a large cage sitting on a stool next to an empty refrigerator. A doctor's scale is next to her. A sign I WILL EAT NO FAT hangs behind her head. She is emaciated, so weak she can't stand. Is this a joke? Jeff asks. Rose points to a smaller sign at the hunger artist's bony foot:

> *I have to fast, I can do nothing else . . . because I could not find the food I like. If I had found it, believe me, I wouldn't have made a fuss but eaten my fill like you and anyone else.*
> —Franz Kafka

Paige chooses a path, under protest. Now she doesn't really have words for what's happening, or isn't actually happening, and she can't make it conform to logic. It has its own logic and is indifferent to reality. She's moving and she's not, she's talking and she's not. Nothing dies here, she hears again.

Maybe something's dead in me, Paige says mournfully.

Nothing's dead in you, it's only unavailable. Behind one object lies another, nothing is lost. Life is a veil . . .

A vale of tears? Paige interrupts.

Life is a veil of self-consciousness, there are many . . .

Many lives? she asks, hopefully.

You have many possibilities, positions, and poses.

I'm a fake?

There are no disguises. Everything reveals you.

Paige struggles with the riddle and the eccentricity of the riddler. Finally she speaks, but her voice cracks, and she doesn't really have control over it. She thinks it's not hers.

"I want to go where I'm not supposed to go. I want to see what I'm not supposed to see. I want what I'm not supposed to have. I want to have everything, before I die. I want to be everything. I don't want life to end, and I don't want it to be for nothing, at the end. I want something about me to live forever. I want death to lose, I don't want to reach an end. I don't want to come to a conclusion. I want to continue. And I don't want anything in my way."

Steve sells tickets for another freak show, it's hardcore, underground, more expensive. In a back room, people slash and cut themselves with razors and hang weights from their nipples or scrotums or both. There's a bondage and whipping act. Marrieds with children don't usually know about this show. It's word of mouth. Steve wants to have his nipples pierced, but he's afraid of blood and disease. He might do it anyway. Della, the dominatrix in this sideshow, knows how to pierce skin antiseptically and without pain. Yesterday, she told him, "Unless you want pain. My slave did." Steve asked, "How can you stand to watch his pain?" Della the dominatrix fixed her eyes on him and answered sternly, "It's not my pain." Steve was rocked by her frankness, her brutality.

Today he sways with abandon to the beat of the inside-out world he frequents. He doesn't think he wants pain or punishment, but he always feels guilty.

Lily Lee and Frank buy tickets to the back room show. Steve thinks Frank looks familiar. But is he a mark or a narc? Frank figures if Lily Lee can accept him, if he lets her know the worst about him, he can marry her without feeling like the pig he is. Frank's lied all his life and thinks everyone's a liar. Besides he's good at it, and it's an occupational hazard. Lily Lee looks at Frank. She likes his paunch. His excess. Lily Lee wants nothing more than to live dangerously. Frank's her ticket to ride. He's a dark character. But she has secrets she'd never tell Frank. She has more sides to her than he could guess.

Lily Lee's mouth drops open. A guy is pounding a spike through his penis. Frank gapes at a man hanging from the ceiling by his tongue. Surprisingly, Frank is sick to his stomach. Lily Lee remembers, with a pang, that she had another dream. In it she handed a hard-boiled egg to Frank. But the yolk wasn't very hard. Maybe she'd tell Frank. He'd probably laugh and say it was a bad dream or bad yolk, that he's a rotten egg. Maybe she does want children.

THE IMPERFECT PRETENSE

Paige isn't sure if she's babbling, in a trance, or daydreaming.

I shouldn't be telling you this, she says aloud.

I may or may not stop you, the old man says. Though you're the one who does that. You may want me to stop you.

No, I don't.

There's no no here.

This is crazy.

You imagine there's something else.

Paige is falling. Like Alice. She refuses to be Alice. She's falling anyway.

She is nowhere she knows. She may lose hope and lose hopelessness, abandon innocence and find her guilt, speak lies and truth, know reason as unreason, discover thoughtful thoughtlessness, and meaning's meaninglessness, be good and bad, and she may uncover things or bury things, forget to forget or forget to remember, and she may deny the dead, embrace hate and love murderousness, she may rage and covet. All her passions are allowed. She may repeat herself, endlessly. She can hold on and hold on, resist nothing, everything, and defend herself constantly.

Paige grips the arms of her chair.

Paige, the old man says, ugliness turns into beauty the way grapes turn into wine, and beauty may be ugly in a bad light.

Grapes aren't ugly, Paige answers, feeling dumb.

Paige is crestfallen, downcast suddenly, and Dr. Joy lifts up her chin. She doesn't know he's doing this. She hears him say: If you don't look for confirmation of your beliefs you'll have an interesting life.

Now Paige imagines he's opened a fortune cookie.

Jeff, Rose, and Kelly emerge from the Odditorium. Rose can't get over the emaciated woman. She's starving herself to death. Kelly awakens and cries out, carousel, I want carousel. Jeff smiles at his demanding little daughter. They follow the signs and walk in the direction of the carousel. Secretly Jeff wishes there'd been a snake woman and a fat man.

The sun is going down, it's cooler, but it's also warm too, balmy, and far above, a mirror to the carnival, the sky is flecked with pink, orange, red, and gold. The sky's on fire. Brilliantly decorated and brightly colored vans and trailers are converging into the center where the carousel acts like a magnet.

Suddenly Jeff and Rose are energetic. The pounding in Jeff's head evaporates, Rose stops worrying about a case she's handling, about the argument she has to make in court the next day, she stops fretting about Jeff.

Paige, wake up, you'll be as awake as you can be. You may remember that you are alone and not alone and that something lives you can never know or grasp fully. This is yours, but it's not yours alone.

Paige wake up.

Paige opens her eyes and senses, weirdly, gravely, that she is awake, that she wasn't completely asleep. She shakes her legs and arms. She imagines she's a dancer and a dance. She knows she's dancing around herself. That's strange, she thinks, I'm not a very good dancer.

Her eyes are wide open.

Paige asks, Am I alone?

Paige, you've come late to your vanity.

What does he mean? she wonders.

I can't see it, she says.

Dr. Joy smiles, then he responds in such a low voice, she can barely hear him. She thinks he says, How can you see all of what's indefinitely, even infinitely, unfinished, with or without you? He pauses and chortles. You and I are easily undone, Paige. And, anyway, seeing isn't believing.

Paige doesn't believe her ears, either.

With Kelly still in his arms, Jeff and Rose keep walking to the carousel. Kelly's beside herself with joy. Streams of people are going their way. Everyone's drinking and eating, giggling and shrieking. Thousands of people are marching in time to organ music. Maybe it's piped in through a public address system coming from the carousel. Jeff isn't sure.

People are wearing silly clothes. People are walking on their hands. People have stockings pulled over their faces as if they're bank robbers. Women are dressed as outrageous men, and men as sensible women, and children are wearing oversized evening

gowns and tuxedos. In a sideshow parade, that's what Rose calls
it, a carnival king and queen are crowned and then their crowns
are stolen from their heads. They're throned and dethroned in a
bizarre celebration. Their chairs are pulled out from under them
again and again, as they're mocked and they mock each other.
People shout, Death to the Dead. Death to the Dead. Death to the
Queen. Death to the King.

Rose knows if they yelled Death to the President, they'd all
be arrested.

Then, Jeff and Rose buy tickets for the carousel from a woman
who claims to be president. President of what? Rose asks the old
woman. Had she penetrated Rose's mind? Of these disunited
states, the old woman answers. The elderly ticket taker smiles
wickedly and turns a cartwheel. I'm eighty, she claims with
glee. Jeff guesses the woman's a gypsy and touches his pocket,
unconsciously. The old woman watches him do it.

Lily Lee and Frank eat hot dogs and drink beer. When the cotton
candy melts in her mouth, she knows she's on earth again. Terra
firma, Frank says, nothing like it. Frank has mustard on his lip, and
Lily Lee wipes it off with her hand. Maybe she really loves him. It's
hard to tell. She's always been romantic, ever since she was a kid and
fell for her first movie star and dreamed about him every night. Rock
Hudson. Every night she prayed to god that he'd bring her Rock.

Paige is ready to leave. She turns to the old man once more.

"You didn't read my mind," she says. Paige is perplexed.

"Mind reading isn't my field. I told you I predict the past."

"That doesn't make sense," Paige objects.

"It doesn't," the old man agrees. "You were reading your own mind. I was listening."

THE FUTURE OF HISTORY

By now Kelly has climbed out of her father's arms. Rose, Jeff, and Kelly linger at the base of the antique carousel. It's red, blue, silver, and green; the sturdy old wooden horses are white, pink, and black. The carousel goes round and round, round and round, round and round so fast, the whirling structure is a blast and blur as the colors whip into one. But then it slows down, goes slower and slower, and figures appear and shapes become objects, and the colors separate again.

Now the three walk on, Kelly and Jeff choose a pink horse, Rose a black horse. The music starts up and the carousel begins to move, and slowly it gains speed. The sturdy horses ascend their poles and descend, they go up and down, up and down, up and down, in time to the music. Kelly is ecstatic. The carousel turns round and round, faster and faster, the music is loud and familiar, people reach for the gold ring, and Rose is floating above herself, above the world. She's flying. She feels she can do anything. She wishes she were still a kid, but not the one she was when she was a kid.

Suddenly, Rose notices a man with a gun. She always sees things like that, evidence like that. He's packing, she says aloud, and reaches across her horse to touch Jeff's arm.

His act is magic, Paige decides. Aware and unaware, and reluctant, she leaves the fortune teller's pink-striped tent just the way she came. She's not sure it's the same passageway. Does he have a license to do this? Paige wonders. She's a little dizzy, almost nauseated. What's magic? she thinks. Maybe nothing really happened.

Steve Whitehurst asks to be relieved. He wants to leave the booth. He doesn't want to work anymore. He wants to be part of the crowd. Besides, he just saw the redhead leave. He has to find her. He wants to drift with her through the Soul Tunnel of Love.

Steve follows Paige. She's unaware of him, she's still in another world. To Steve she looks blissed out. What if, he thinks, I kissed her, the way the soldier kissed the woman in Times Square? That famous end-of-the-war photograph had impressed Steve when he was a kid. It happened on your birthday, his mother told him proudly. Why not? Steve thinks.

In the distance people scream on the roller coaster. Steve realizes his life has been one long ride on an emotional roller coaster.

Lily Lee and Frank stroll along Lovers' and Others' Lane. She has agreed to marry him. She agreed one time before, but she left the man standing at the altar. The morning of the wedding, she awoke and couldn't move. The doctor called it temporary paralysis. Her mother said, You didn't want to marry him. Lily Lee prays that doesn't happen again.

They walk aimlessly and arrive at the carousel. Lily Lee wants to grab a ride. Frank reluctantly nods yes. To him it's silly. They buy tickets from the woman who claims to be president. Now her clothes are on, inside out.

So many people are around, more and more of them. It's working my nerves, Frank tells Lily Lee. He hates crowds, crowds worry him, the possibility of danger and disaster. Frank touches the gun under his belt, the bulge on his right hip. His gun never leaves his side.

Just then a huge float passes by. It's painted red, draped with shiny red satin, and lit by Chinese lanterns adorned with crystal spangles. On the side of it is a sign: HELL. Frank nudges Lily Lee, See, baby, now we can go to hell together.

Paige drifts and weaves through the crowd. Steve is near her, following her, but he's also caught up in the makeshift parade. Some acrobats join the throng and turn cartwheels. Dancers in pink tights and toe shoes stand on their toes. Everyone glides along to the canny rhythm of the organ music. The red float named Hell passes Paige too. Comic red devils leap up and down on the top of the float. They stick their tongues out and cry Death to the Father. Paige touches her red hair. Nothing ever dies, she remembers. The devils point at each other ironically and shout: Death to You. Death to You.

Steve gathers up his courage. He moves closer to Paige and introduces himself, and no, he doesn't kiss her, he simply says, Isn't this weird? Paige nods.

Then she sees Dr. Joy. She thinks it's him, anyway. He's dressed as a clown, with a fright wig, red lipstick dotted on his cheeks and an enormous, painted-green mouth. Dr. Joy spots her, signals, and stands on his head. Everything's upside down, Paige exclaims to Steve. Steve puts his arm around her, as if to steady her, but really he's steadying himself. He wants her.

Rose, Jeff, Kelly, Frank, and Lily Lee are going round and round on the carousel, round and round and up and down. Turning and turning, even Frank is subdued, nearly content. Things seem possible and unpredictable. Kelly grabs a ring, Jeff kisses Rose, Frank starts to get emotional, and Lily Lee cries for no reason. There seems to be no need for restraint.

Then, suddenly, there's a noise, a huge roar, an explosion, and the float named Hell goes up in flames. The fire rises and burns wildly, grandly, it's out of control, it's not being controlled, and the red satin cloth, the Chinese lanterns, everything is immolated in its glorious blaze. No one's afraid. People cheer, joke, dance, and laugh, as if tomorrow will never come.

Paige is ready for anything. Craziness has erupted, and she's carrying weird, anarchic instructions. Don't look for confirmation, you can't see, you're undone . . .

Steve's almost naked with his longing and lust stains his blue eyes. Paige wants him to want her. His desire is a delicacy on her plate for her. The heat in his eyes turns them liquid and silky, empty of everything. He has an illusion of her, of what she could be. She sees that. He might be disappointed. There's always disappointment and regret, and Paige wants regret less than she wants to want anything. His heart beats under his shirt. Paige likes that.

Later, when Steve and Paige ride through the Soul Tunnel of Love, she relishes the anonymity of being a stranger, the fantasy of being strange with a stranger.

Eventually, though the fire still burns and the shouts and laughter continue, Frank becomes aware of the man with the gun. It pulls him from one world into another. The man touches his gun so Frank draws his. He shouts: Police officer. The man fires, and they exchange shots. Rose is hit in the shoulder by the round of bullets. She isn't seriously hurt, but the dramatic event will change the course of her life. Kelly's in shock, startled by the sight of blood, the sound of gunfire, the confusion around her. She howls. For hours she's inconsolable.

In what seems only a few breathless seconds, Rose is rushed to the hospital, and Jeff, with Kelly crying in his arms, accompanies her in the ambulance. Frank and Lily Lee are escorted by two cops, who know Frank, to the nearest police station. The unknown man, the assailant with the gun, gets away. He loses himself in the carnival crowd. The cops pick him up later. His gun's registered to his brother.

THE PAST IS TENSE

Lily Lee didn't leave Frank at the altar. One night, though, shortly after their marriage, Frank went berserk and threatened to kill himself. Lily Lee insisted he get counseling or she'd divorce him. They never had children. She wanted a dog and finally bought one.

Rose dissolved her partnership with Jeff, gave up law, and moved to New Mexico. She fell in love with a dancer named Gwen and, one day, opened a storefront law office. She couldn't stay away from it.

Jeff reunited with his wife for a while, then they separated again for good. He became an expert in DNA, and in his spare time read about extinct forms of life. For years he worried about Kelly's future.

Kelly wanted to be a musician and played in a few groups around town. For a couple of years she had a drug problem. Jeff thought it was the result of the divorce, even the trauma of the gunfire at the carnival. Kelly thought it was about being the child of a mixed marriage in a racist country. She overcame her drug problem and studied art history. Kelly focused on color, its meanings and interpretations, aesthetic and cultural, in contemporary theory and history.

Paige and Steve had a torrid and occasionally torporific relationship. They played in ways she and he had never before tried or done. To both of them their involvement was extreme, exhausting, but it was an accomplishment, achieved against overwhelming odds.

Out of the blue, Paige broke up with Steve. By way of explaining, she wrote him a letter:

"I liked your following me. Ordinarily I wouldn't have, I don't think. That carnival deranged me, rearranged me maybe. It was a good and a bad start for us. You don't know where you're standing when you're with me, you said. I didn't know where you stood in my scheme of things. I know I shouldn't have a scheme of things, but I do. Dr. Joy was a joke, you said, but he wasn't funny. I couldn't take it all in, and I couldn't take in you and your scene, and my decisions along the way made it hard for me to deal with yours. There's no way to apprehend or appreciate everything about anyone else. I'm selfish or just limited like everyone else, or both. I didn't see the end coming, I couldn't. Then one day I didn't feel for you. I'm giving you my version. I don't want to defend myself, and I know I am. It was chance. I'm just what you met that day. This is what I made of things. You kidded me about how it was bigger than both of us. It was. You and I nearly believed and then I stopped believing. I want to believe in what can't be seen in the moments I'm not there. But I don't have confidence. Maybe we were just hanging out. And in the end there was my ambivalence, my mixed feelings, as you used to say, always there, and where we started from and what I brought with me. . . ."

Paige never finished the letter. In her mind she addressed it to Steve, but it wasn't really for him. What she had told him, the last time they met, was: It was a fantasy, and now it's not anymore. I don't know what it is. I'm sorry.

The next day Steve had his nipples pierced and for about a year was one of Della's slaves. Then he lost interest in Della, quit the carnival, and wistfully thought about becoming a priest and taking a vow of celibacy. But he didn't. Instead Steve learned the computer software business. To his good friends Frank and Lily Lee—they'd met at an s&m party—Steve cracked inside jokes about hardware and software, of the hard and soft wear and tear on his life.

ONCE UPON A TIME AGAIN

Forever after, Paige Turner pondered the wonderful and disquieting events of the strange day and night at the carnival. It became a turning point for her, one she never completely understood. She couldn't explain it to herself or anyone else. She often dwelled on the sensations of losing herself, and not losing herself, or being herself and not caring who she was, of having been in a trance or hypnotized, of standing in a place out of place, of not seeing and seeing, of being frightened and calm, and all this was familiar and mysterious. She never forgave herself for the way she broke up with Steve and worried, long after his face was a dead letter, whether she'd used him.

Over the years Paige discovered she'd memorized the day and night at the carnival. The details were kept in her mind, like precious objects in a box. She mentioned the day more and more, at odd moments too. Occasionally she embellished it, and sometimes she chose new words to describe it. Sometimes she said it was indescribable and indefinable, but she never believed that. And sometimes a detail imposed itself, one that she hadn't remembered the last time. The telling of the tale came to have the character of a fable or myth, whose truth or falsehood was hers to cherish.

And much, much later, when years had passed, many years, and she was very old, and her red hair was white, and not long before she died, when the events of every day and every night merged together, when every thought was liminal, and every conversation the remnant of a hypnagogic dream, Paige strained to live the day and night again fully, even to read her mind. Her mind wandered. It might never have happened. Not that way, not that way, that way, yes, that way, I believe, yes, yes, I think it must have been that way, it might have, yes, like that, yes.

And so, to the end, Paige held the thrill close, like an old friend.

Acknowledgments

I want to thank all of the artists in this collection who asked me to write for their artists' books or catalogues, and who, even when I explained that I would write fiction, let me go ahead. Over the years, talking with the twenty-two artists represented, and others with whom I have yet to work, has enabled me to think about contemporary art from the point of view of conceptualizing and producing it. I also want to thank their galleries, and the museums and other institutions, magazines and journals that have commissioned my writing.

I'd also like to acknowledge Doug Ohlson and Ron Gorchov, with whom I studied painting and watercolor when I was an undergraduate at Hunter College. Learning about it from doing it trained me to think about art differently, and writing fiction as an analogue to art seemed an outgrowth of practicing it. Also, their bemused, supportive attitude toward the only English major in the art department was strangely encouraging. It was Hope Ruff who urged me to take painting classes, and I thank her for that. I'd like to thank the MacDowell Colony for being that quiet place where I can write, undisturbed.

And to those who made this book an actuality: Sharon Gallagher, its publisher, who immediately wanted to do it and whose support and ideas for it were amazing; Lori Waxman, its editor, with whom everything could be discussed and who understood instantly, and whose intelligence also shaped this book, and Carole Goodman, its designer, whose original, beautiful design thrills me, thank you so much. To all the others at D.A.P., especially Alex Galan, who cheerleaded its publicity, my gratitude. All of you have made a dream come true.

Credits

This is the first publication of any kind for the novella *Come and Go*, the story "The Undiagnosed," and the series of short stories entitled "Hold Me." The majority of the other stories have appeared only in very limited edition artist portfolios or artists' books, or in museum or gallery catalogues.

"Dead Sleep," in *Dormir/Sleep*, Coromandel Press, Paris: 2000. "Flowers," in *Flowers*, with Vik Muniz, limited edition portfolio [50 copies], Coromandel Press, Paris: 1999. *Living with Contradictions*, drawings by Jane Dickson, New York: Top Stories, 1982."The Lost City of Words," in *Still Lives*, with Kiki Smith, limited edition portfolio [60 copies], Coromandel Press, Paris: 2002. "Lust for Loss: Back to the Front," in *Tourisms of War*, ed. Diller = Scofidio, Normandie: F.R.A.C. Basse, 1994. *Madame Realism*, drawings by Kiki Smith, New York: LINE grant, 1984. "Madame Realism Lies Here," in *Here Lies*, ed. Karl Roeseler and David Gilbert, Trip Street Press, San Francisco: 2001. "Madame Realism Looks for Relief," in *Haim Steinbach*, Castello di Rivoli, Edizioni Charta, Milan: 1995. "Madame Realism: A Fairy Tale," in *Silvia Kolbowski XI Projects*, New York: Border Editions, 1988. "Madame Realism's Torch Song," in *Marco Breuer SMTWTFS*, a limited edition, PPP Editions in association with Roth Horowitz LLC, New York: 2002. "Ode to le Petomane", in *Roni Horn: Gurgles Sucks Echoes*, New York: Matthew Marks, February 1995; Koln: Jablonka Galerie. "Phantoms," an extensively revised version of "Still Lives," in *Laura Letinsky*, Chicago: The Museum of Contemporary Photography, Columbia College, 1997. "A Picture of Time," in *Stephen Ellis: Paintings*, Edition Lintel & Nusser; and first published in *Ploughshares*, ed. Paul Muldoon, Vol. 6, No. 1, Boston: Spring 2000. "Pleasure Isn't A Pretty Picture," in *Head Shots*, photographs by Aura Rosenberg, New York: Stopover Press, 1996. "Snow-Job," in *Seduce*, Coromandel Press, Paris: 2002. "This Is Not It," in *Silence Please! Stories after the works of Juan Muñoz*, eds. Juan Muñoz, Louise Neri, James Lingwood, Dublin: Irish Museum of Modern Art/Berlin-New York: Scalo, 1996. "Thrilled to Death," in *Jessica Stockholder: Your Skin in this Weatherbourne Eye-Threads&Swollen Perfume*, New York: DIA, 1996. "To Find Words" (novella), in *Serious Hysterics*, London: Serpent's Tail, 1992. "TV Tales" (originally called "21 TV Tales"), in *Barbara Kruger*, Melbourne: Museum of Modern Art at Heide, 1996. "Wild Life" (A Portfolio for Barbara Ess), *Annandale*, Bard College: Spring 1998.

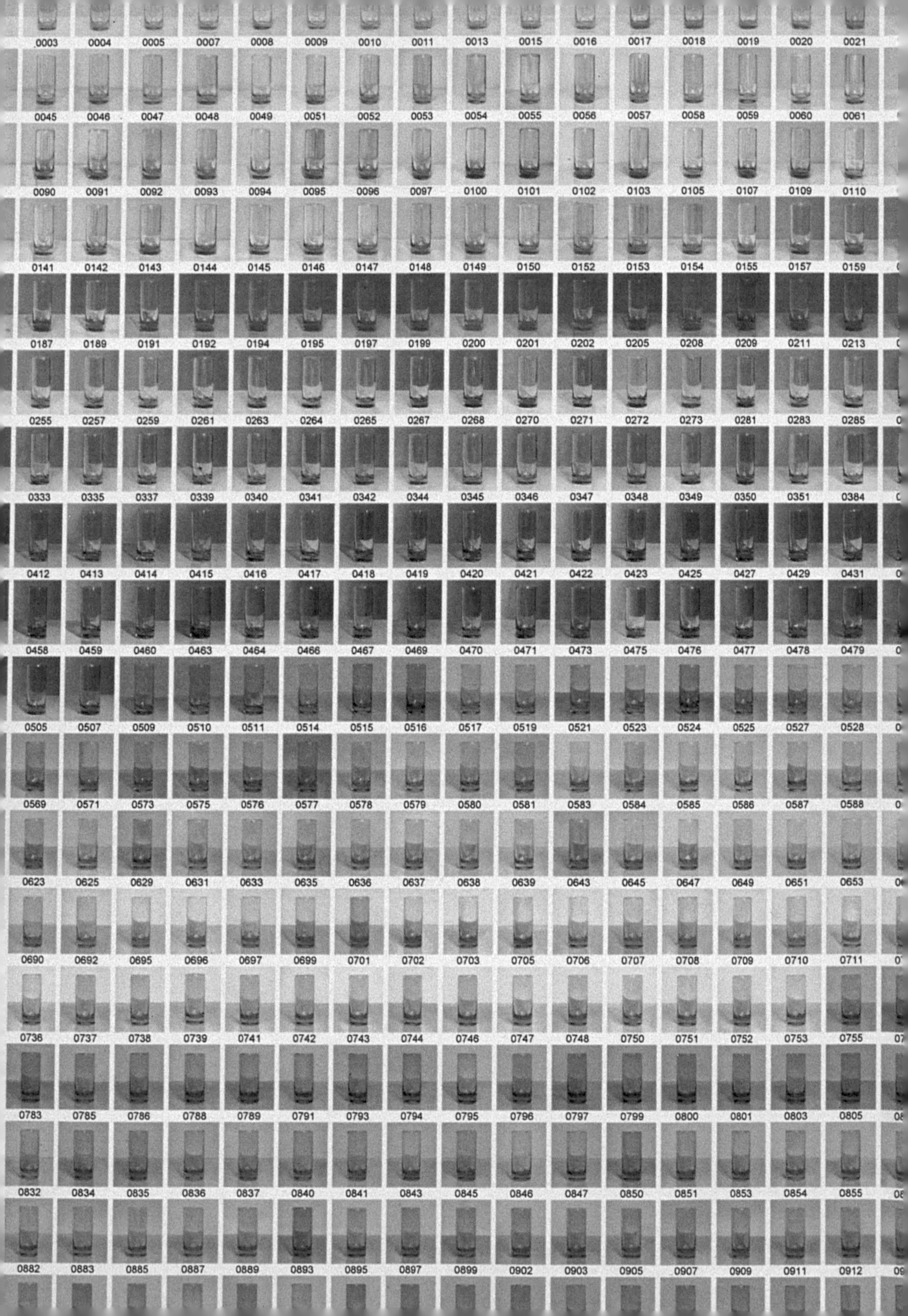
0003 0004 0005 0007 0008 0009 0010 0011 0013 0015 0016 0017 0018 0019 0020 0021
0045 0046 0047 0048 0049 0051 0052 0053 0054 0055 0056 0057 0058 0059 0060 0061
0090 0091 0092 0093 0094 0095 0096 0097 0100 0101 0102 0103 0105 0107 0109 0110
0141 0142 0143 0144 0145 0146 0147 0148 0149 0150 0152 0153 0154 0155 0157 0159
0187 0189 0191 0192 0194 0195 0197 0199 0200 0201 0202 0205 0208 0209 0211 0213
0255 0257 0259 0261 0263 0264 0265 0267 0268 0270 0271 0272 0273 0281 0283 0285
0333 0335 0337 0339 0340 0341 0342 0344 0345 0346 0347 0348 0349 0350 0351 0384
0412 0413 0414 0415 0416 0417 0418 0419 0420 0421 0422 0423 0425 0427 0429 0431
0458 0459 0460 0463 0464 0466 0467 0469 0470 0471 0473 0475 0476 0477 0478 0479
0505 0507 0509 0510 0511 0514 0515 0516 0517 0519 0521 0523 0524 0525 0527 0528
0569 0571 0573 0575 0576 0577 0578 0579 0580 0581 0583 0584 0585 0586 0587 0588
0623 0625 0629 0631 0633 0635 0636 0637 0638 0639 0643 0645 0647 0649 0651 0653
0690 0692 0695 0696 0697 0699 0701 0702 0703 0705 0706 0707 0708 0709 0710 0711
0736 0737 0738 0739 0741 0742 0743 0744 0746 0747 0748 0750 0751 0752 0753 0755
0783 0785 0786 0788 0789 0791 0793 0794 0795 0796 0797 0799 0800 0801 0803 0805
0832 0834 0835 0836 0837 0840 0841 0843 0845 0846 0847 0850 0851 0853 0854 0855
0882 0883 0885 0887 0889 0893 0895 0897 0899 0902 0903 0905 0907 0909 0911 0912